SHINE ON, OKLAHOMA
THE MCINTYRE MEN
BOOK FOUR

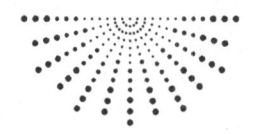

MAGGIE SHAYNE

All rights reserved.

No part of this publication may be sold, copied, distributed, reproduced or transmitted in any form or by any means, mechanical or digital, including photocopying and recording or by any information storage and retrieval system without the prior written permission of both the publisher, Oliver Heber Books and the author, Maggie Shayne, except in the case of brief quotations embodied in critical articles and reviews.

PUBLISHER'S NOTE: This is a work of fiction. Names, characters, places, and incidents either are the product of the author's imagination or are used fictitiously. Any resemblance to actual persons, living or dead, business establishments, events, or locales is entirely coincidental.

Copyright 2017 by Margaret S. Lewis

Edited by Jena O'Connor, Practical Proofing

Published by Oliver-Heber Books

0 9 8 7 6 5 4 3 2 1

❀ Created with Vellum

I dedicate this book to Carolyn Hanlon, aka Carolyn Andrews, aka Cara Summers. I got the last word on Lieutenant Mendoza. But I hooked you up. You're welcome. I've heard your laughter inside my head the whole time. You are missed, but I know you're not far. See you, my friend.

CHAPTER ONE

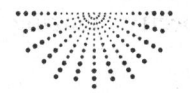

Dax Russell hit the double doors running, only to be met by a nurse and an orderly. The alarm on their faces let him know he was out of line.

He took a step back, held up his hands. "Sorry." He was out of breath, had run all the way from the taxi. Then he saw his mom, just coming out of a hospital room through a heavy wood door that dwarfed her. Caroline Russell was Tinkerbell personified, and he adored her.

She met his eyes, gave him a sad smile and then said to the staff standing between them, "It's okay. That's our son."

"Oh. Thank God." The nurse patted his chest, and the orderly grinned and shook his head as they moved aside. Dax met his mom halfway. Her pixie short platinum hair was probably mostly silver now, but you couldn't really tell with blond hair that light. She hugged him and he picked her up off her feet like he always did when he saw her. It was kind of their thing, him being so big, her being so small. He hugged her hard, but not too hard, then set her on her little feet again.

It often amazed him that a man of his size had somehow been produced by a little thing like his mom.

"How are you, honey?" she asked.

He lifted his head and looked toward the door she'd come out of. "I'll let you know."

"No, tell me now. How *are* you?"

The way she said it, he knew what she was asking. And he didn't mind. "Dry since Christmas," he said. "Not a drop."

"And?"

He smiled. "Life is pretty amazing when your eyeballs are clear enough to see it."

"It is."

It wasn't. The only woman he'd ever loved was a criminal, and he couldn't seem to get over her. But that wasn't anything his mother needed to know.

She took him by the hand, led him in the wrong direction.

He tugged half-heartedly. "I should see him."

"After we talk." She led him through the ICU, through a set of doors and into a small waiting room with little round tables and padded chairs. A TV set mounted high on one ivory wall played the headlines to no audience. A row of vending machines, a row of windows, and a water cooler filled the remaining wall space.

Caroline went to a little table far from the television, near the windows. Dax sat down, and she did too, and then she clasped his hand in both of hers across the table. "It's your father's time honey," she said. "The cardiologist is amazed he even made it to the hospital. It was a massive heart attack."

It seemed like her words didn't register in his brain at first. She could read him, his mom could. She loved him, had left her boorish husband mostly because of him, he'd always thought. His father was a bully, and it didn't matter if you were a business rival or his own son. He was mean to everyone. And yet she was here. Probably because there was no one else who cared enough to be bothered.

"He's going to die," she said. "Do you understand, Dax?"

"He's gonna die?"

"Yes. I'm sorry, son."

He blinked, trying to find words. His father was a strapping, powerful man. He couldn't just die. "When?"

"Could be any minute. Could be a couple of days. The doctor says it won't be longer. Right now, he's slipping in and out of consciousness. Eventually, he'll just slip out and keep on going."

"Wh-what about life support? Why can't they keep him—"

"There's too much damage to his heart, Dax. He'd need a transplant, but there's damage to other organs, as well, and his lifetime of drinking has riddled his liver. There's no way back from this."

He blinked, taking that in. It sounded cold, somehow. "Can I see him now?" he asked, staring at nothing, a spot in the space between them.

She nodded and let go of his hand. "I'll be right here."

He got to his feet and walked mindlessly out of the waiting room. A nurse saw him, the one who'd stopped him in the hall, and gave a smile. He had brown hair and bangs that tried to cover up the acne on his forehead, and his eyes were soft but knowing. He pointed at the door, and said, "three-oh-five" in a funeral voice.

Dax pushed the door open and went inside. At first he thought he'd walked into the wrong room. A wrinkled, saggy-faced man with gray tinted skin lay against white sheets, beneath a white blanket. The top sheet was folded over the blanket, and the old man's arms were resting on top of it. There was an IV line in his arm, and oxygen tubes in his nostrils. There were leads strung from his chest to a monitor. The monitor and IV were mounted to a pole beside the bed. The oxygen came from a port on the wall.

His hair was mostly white, but streaks of carrot-stained

yellow still showed through. That was what told Dax he wasn't in the wrong room, those faded orange streaks. Only he used to have a lot more of them.

When did he get so old?

Dax sank into a bedside chair and remembered the last time he'd spoken to his father. He'd admitted that he'd taken money from the Aurora Downs accounts to give to a beautiful con artist for a kidney transplant she didn't really need. He'd paid it back, thanks to a loan from a friend. But that hadn't mattered to his father. He'd fired him on the spot, called him six kinds of idiot, and disowned him.

That had been eighteen months ago.

Mom was sure he'd been sorry after. She thought Dax ought to come home and talk it out. But he knew better. Dax had apologized three times, deeply and sincerely, in voicemails left on his father's cell, because the old man wouldn't take his calls. But admitting he'd been even a little bit wrong was beneath the great man. In fact, sitting there, Dax couldn't recall ever hearing his father apologize to anyone in his whole life. Still, he wished they'd made peace, him and Dad, before it came to this.

"I thought there'd be more time." Dax said it softly, turning away, blinking back tears. He focused on the monitor instead of the man, studied its wavy lines and numbers as if he had a clue what they meant.

"*Now* you show up."

Dax turned fast, saw that the old man's eyes were open, watery and bloodshot, the white parts tarnished. "Dad." He moved closer, patted a big hand with his own. "I'm here."

His father grimaced, then his eyes fell closed. "I thought so, too," he said.

"Thought what, too?" Dax recalled his own words. "That there'd be more time?"

His father nodded.

"It doesn't matter now, Dad. It's all good, all is forgiven."

Those dull eyes popped open with near violent force and his head came right off the pillow. *"Forgiven?"* There was no mistaking the disgust in his voice. Then he let his head fall back onto the pillows again. "Nothing is forgiven. I thought there'd be more time to change my will. Too late now, though."

Dax stood up slow, knowing now that this wasn't going to be the moment he'd wanted it to be. No mending of the rift, no healing moment, no tender goodbye. He was stupid to have thought it could be like that. Then he took a deep breath. "I'm sorry about what I did. I honestly thought Kendra's life depended on it."

"She played you."

"It's what she does." He shrugged. "I thought you'd want to make peace with your only son before you died. I thought you'd want a chance to say goodbye."

His father closed his eyes. "Try not to fuck up my legacy like you fuck up everything else."

It stung. It shouldn't have. He'd hardened his heart against his old man years ago. And yet it stung. "If you left it to me, you can forget it. I don't want it."

His father's eyes opened a little wider. "You refuse it, it goes to the SRA."

"I don't care. Let the State Racing Association have it."

"But your mother…"

"Owns forty-nine percent. I know. She can do what she wants with her half. It has nothing to do with me." He started to turn away, but a hand gripped his wrist with surprising strength. He turned back. His father's face wasn't white, it was red, bordering on purple, his eyes bulging.

"She'll go to prison."

Dax widened his eyes. "What did you do, Dad?"

"SRA…the books…" He relaxed all at once. His eyes fell closed.

Dax swore, and bent over his father, clasped his shoulders. "What about the books? Dad! Dad!"

His father didn't reply. His face didn't look strained anymore. It was relaxed. Dax shot a look at the monitor. Its lines had gone flat.

CHAPTER TWO

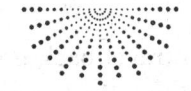

FOUR DAYS LATER...

"Hey, Dax. How you doin'?"

His spine went rigid. Her familiar, sexy-as-hell voice raked his nerve endings like a red-hot dagger. *Kendra.*

He was sitting at The Long Branch, sipping a giant mug of foamy, icy root beer, mainly just to prove to himself that he could. And for the company. Jason McIntyre was manning the bar this morning, helping out because the owner, his brother Joey, was too busy with his pet project, The Twig.

Jason met Dax's eyes over the bar. They offered support, should he need it. Then he wandered to the other end of the bar to give them space.

The place was dead, but it was early. Its curved hardwood bar gleamed, and the tables around the room were mostly empty. The player piano was silent. Just past the curving staircase that led up to several guest rooms, red velvet curtains hung, graceful and heavy and soft. The dining room was on the other side, but that half of the place wasn't open this early in the day.

Bracing himself, Dax spun his saddle-shaped barstool around to face her.

And there she was. He looked from her big, emerald green

eyes, as innocent as springtime, to her plump, lonely lips, to the ivory silk cami that clung to her breasts and didn't quite reach to the top of her low-slung, skin-tight jeans. She wore a denim jacket over the top, unbuttoned, and high heeled boots under the jeans.

He knew every inch of her. He'd loved her. Planned to marry her. She'd scammed him out of a pile of money and left him in the dust.

He forced his eyes to travel back up to her face again. Her hair wasn't strawberry blond like her twin sister Kiley's. It was lighter, the color of sweet lemonade, and long, and perfectly straight.

"Hello, Kendra." He tried to make it sound cold and distant, and to hide the parts of him that wanted to lurch off the stool, pick her up and kiss her until she quivered. "What brings you back to Big Falls?"

"I miss my sister."

Her sister. Hell. "She uh…she know you're coming?"

"I imagine she does by now," she said, giving a little nod. He followed her gaze and saw Jason, just sliding his phone back into his pocket.

He knew better than to take anything Kendra said as the truth, though. As a general rule, if her mouth was open and sounds were coming out, she was lying.

"You came here first?" If she was really in town to see Kiley, what was she doing at The Long Branch?

"Thought I'd see if I could get a room, unload my crap, freshen up. I don't want Kiley to feel like she has to put me up."

"I see." No, he didn't.

She lowered her thick lashes until they touched her cheeks. "I heard about your father, Dax. I'm real sorry."

"How?" he asked.

"How what?" Her eyes opened again, locked onto his. "How did I hear?"

He nodded.

"Online, I guess. A friend of mine who knows a friend of yours posted an RIP or something like that."

"Something like that."

She nodded. "That why you're drinking? Last I knew you were on the wagon."

He said, "Yep. Drowning my sorrows in root beer."

She blinked, her green eyes sliding to the mug. Then she smiled and it was the first genuine expression he'd seen cross her face so far. "That's great. I'm glad." She slid up onto a stool beside him. Jason noticed and came right over. Kendra's twin sister Kiley was married to Jason's brother Rob, so technically, they were family.

"Hey, Kendra. What can I get you?"

"I'll have what he's having," she said. "And some information."

Jason and Dax exchanged a quick look that said, *here it comes*.

"I'm dying to know what on earth you McIntyres are up to out yonder?" She gestured left, in the general direction of the construction project. It was fifty yards east and twenty yards back from the road, on Long Branch land. Another fifty yards past that was Joe and Emily's newly built home.

"Joey's building a miniature of The Long Branch out there for kids," Jason said. "Bat-wing doors and all. Inside there'll be a ball pit, arcade, and they'll serve ice cream and pop. Outside, mini-golf and a paintball course."

She lifted her brows and looked to Dax, who nodded confirmation. "Joey bought his brothers out, and he's been going strong ever since. He's calling his new venture The Twig."

She slapped her thigh and laughed. Jason slid a mug of root beer her way.

"He has a wife and a little girl now," Jason said. "You'll meet 'em if you stick around long enough. Did I hear you say you needed a room?"

"Yeah, if you have anything."

He plucked a key off a hook under the bar, slid it across the wood to her. "Top of the stairs, hang a right. Corner room. No charge."

"You don't have to do that. I can pay my own way."

"It's a Brand-McIntyre rule," Jason said. "Family doesn't charge family."

"Not even the black sheep?" she asked.

"Not even," Jason said.

"Thank you. I'm grateful." She took a sip. Foam stuck to her upper lip. Dax wanted to kiss it away, so he looked elsewhere. Then she said, "I feel bad, Dax. I caused a rift between you and your dad."

"You widened a rift that was already there," he said.

"Still..." Deep breath, sincerity in her eyes. A little too much of it. "I hope you had the chance to mend fences before...." She let the words trail off, waited for him to fill in the rest.

"I was with him when he passed," he said. Which really didn't explain anything.

"Are you okay?"

"Yeah. I am."

"You don't seem okay." She sighed, and when he didn't say anything, took another sip. "I'd like to ask you a favor, Dax."

He had no doubt she did. He'd been waiting for her to get to the point, tell him what it was she wanted from him this time around. God knew if she was here and being nice to him, she must want something. "What kind of favor?"

Her deep breath expanded her breasts against the cami. He tried not to notice and noticed anyway. "I don't know how Kiley's gonna feel about me showing up. I'm... would you go out there with me?"

He closed his eyes slowly, opened them again. "I don't get it."

"I know it probably doesn't make a lot of sense to you, but... when we were together—"

"We were never together," he said. "It was just a game you were running."

"I was running a game. But you weren't. You were a great boyfriend. I always felt good about myself when I was with you. I always felt safe."

"You don't feel safe around your sister?"

"I don't feel good about myself around my sister."

That was the thing with Kendra. She'd lie to him, she'd con him, but every once in a while she'd show him her soul in a moment of brutal, undeniable honesty. To this day he didn't think she did that with anyone else. He took a deep breath, sighed heavily. "I have to go over anyway."

"You do?"

"Yeah." He drained his glass. Hers was only half empty. "Give me your keys. I'll get your bags for you while you finish up."

She smiled, a watery, wavery little smile of gratitude and relief. No hint of triumph, like he'd have expected if she thought she had him wrapped around her finger again.

He probably ought to warn her about what she was going to find out at Rob and Kiley's Holiday Ranch. But he decided not to. It wasn't his place. That was a matter between the two sisters. They'd have to work it out on their own.

Kendra dug out her car keys, dangled them in front of him. He took them, looked at them, and said, "You're driving a 'Vette?"

That smile was real. "Sixty-two, red and white drop top. It's my most prized possession."

"I bet it is." He wondered what poor slob she'd taken for such a sweet ride, but he took the keys without asking and headed out to the parking lot to get her bags. Not because he was falling into her sticky, deadly web again, but because he hadn't been raised to tell a girl to go get her own damn bags.

And because he wanted to get a look at that car.

Kendra drove out to the place where she'd grown up playing in wildflower meadows with her twin sister and thinking life would always be just that sweet.

She barely remembered her mother. Kiley didn't either, but she'd built a pretty convincing version in her imagination—equal parts sixties sit-com supermom and angel. But Diana Kellogg hadn't lived to see her twin daughters' fourth birthday, and she couldn't have been too angelic. She'd married Jack, after all.

Kendra's heart twisted up a little as she thought of her father. In her head she saw his smile, the one that could charm the panties off a nun, the deep dimples, the sparkle in his light blue eyes.

He'd better be okay.

She glanced into the rearview mirror. Dax's angry, snarling Charger came right behind, like a bright orange tiger stalking a deer, ironically, driven by the sweetest guy in America. Or at least he used to be. He seemed bitter now, wary, but whose fault was that? She firmed her jaw, caught a gear, pressed harder on the gas.

A few miles west of The Long Branch, she took a right onto Pine Road. She'd never seen the irony in the name until she'd lived in the northeast for a while. You couldn't get five minutes outside NYC before the majestic conifers showed up, carpeting every rolling hill and tall enough to tickle the sky. What passed for a pine tree here was like a New York pine tree's botched GMO experiment. One of the freaky ones that would have to be mercifully put down.

It was different here. Flatter, and wider, and hotter. And the pine trees were crooked and short, like arthritic old men.

The road was familiar, unwinding between wide meadows and harvested fields. The grasses were tall and spotted with orange Indian Paintbrush and yellow dandelions, even in mid-November, all of it swaying in the breeze like a slow-motion dance. The sun hung low. Every now and then, a sunbeam bounced off the Cimarron, at the far edge of the green dancing meadow, and flashed bright yellow in her eyes. It was fall. And she was home.

"What a sentimental pile of horse shit." She turned left into the driveway, under the big HOLIDAY RANCH arch, past the barns, all freshly painted red with white trim. They'd cleared out the barnyard that used to be in front of the smaller barn, dozed it flat and added gravel to make a parking area surrounded by a split rail fence. The big barn had been modified, and looked almost new. There were horses grazing in the fields that stretched between the barns and the river, colts kicking up their heels where Kendra and Kiley used to play.

They'd painted the house too, white with red trim, and a white picket fence surrounded it now.

"It must'a looked so pretty once," a little girl's voice said in her memory. And she was there, right there, near that corner fencepost, with Kiley, who held up a rotted piece of rail that was still clinging by a single nail. "I bet it went all the way around."

"We could fix it, maybe," Kendra had said, her head full of visions of how nice it would look. Visions that had been quickly shattered, when her father put his two cents in. "And how you gonna get the funds for it, Kendra? Who's gonna buy the boards and the nails and the paint? Not me, I'll tell you that. You gotta start thinking about things like this now, so you don't grow up all dependent and needy. You gotta figure out how to make your own way in this world. No one's ever gonna do it for you."

She sighed and snapped her attention back to the present, to the white picket fence around the house, and the shutters with the little heart-shaped cutouts. They'd replaced the old, rotting window boxes with new ones, painted red to match the barn, all of them overflowing with orange and yellow flowers.

It was as pretty as two little girls had once dreamed it could be.

The front door opened, and Kiley came outside. Her belly was as big as a beach ball. Her hands rested on top of it, and its weight pulled her back into a gentle arch.

Kendra hit the clutch and brakes and sat there in a cloud of red Oklahoma dust, staring. "What the—"

A soft *beep beep* from behind made her blink. Swallowing hard, she eased the stick into first gear and found a spot to park.

Her sister was pregnant and she hadn't told her.

Kendra didn't like the way that hurt. She didn't do emotional shit, so it was uncomfortable to feel as if a hot blade had just slipped cleanly between her ribs and right though her heart. A blade held by Kiley. *Kiley!* The *good* twin.

She shut the car off and got out, taking a ridiculous amount of time to adjust her handbag over her shoulder, and clip her keyring into its spot inside.

Then, vaguely aware of the Charger rumbling to a stop nearby and shutting off, and of its door opening and closing again, Kendra walked toward the house where her sister waited.

Kiley looked worried behind her welcome-home smile.

Kendra walked a little faster, her anger like a weighted blanket, laid over the hurt. Anger was much more comfortable to her. No way was she going to let the sunshine, the breeze, and the combined smells of horse, hay, and river sooth her indignation away.

When she got close enough, she stopped, crossed her arms over her chest involuntarily. "How could you not tell me?"

Kiley's smile died. She looked down, looked up again, sighed. "You want to do this now? Don't even want to catch up first? See what we've done with the place? Tell me what you've been up to?"

"Why, Kiley?"

Kiley heaved a sigh. "Because I don't want our father to know she exists."

"She?"

"Yeah. We're having a girl."

And she wasn't going to tell me, Kendra reminded herself, when the idea of a little girl running around this place tried to dissolve her anger by dousing it in buckets of warm gooiness. "She's his granddaughter," Kendra said. "He has a right—"

"He's a criminal. He has no rights. I don't want her growing up like we did, Kendra."

"How could she? She's got Snow White and Prince Charming for parents."

"Don't. Just don't." Kiley held up a stop-sign hand, shaking her head rapidly. "You remember how it was, the kinds of people who were always coming around. We're lucky nothing awful happened."

"Uncle Willie? Fat Carl and Miss Dolly? Those kinds of people?"

"Yeah," Kiley said. "Crooks."

"You used to call them family."

"I didn't know any better."

"You'll *never* know any better. They're salt-of-the-earth people, Kendra."

"Willie robbed banks, Fat Carl hustled tourists."

"And Dolly was always there for us, any time we needed her. She tracked us down at every foster home. She made sure we each got a present every birthday, every Christmas."

Kiley lowered her head. "Dolly's a con. Not a very good one, though." She smiled a little. She'd always had a soft spot for Miss Dolly, and Kendra knew it. "But if she knew, Dad would know."

"Dad isn't so bad that he doesn't deserve to know he has a grandchild."

"Yes, he is, Kendra! You've just always had a blind spot where he's concerned. I've never understood it. You can see right through everyone else, straight to their flaws and hidden motives. But with Dad, you just...you just want him to be a good father so much that you refuse to see he's just...not."

"So what? You're *perfect* now?"

"I'm not gonna have criminals around my daughter."

"And that includes me, right Kiley?"

Kiley lowered her head. "I want you in her life. I do. You're my sister."

"But?"

"But... not if you're gonna keep living like that."

"So you're gonna dictate my life now?"

"No. I just get to dictate my daughter's."

"Yeah. Good luck with that." Kendra turned back toward the car. Dax was standing a few feet behind her, his eyes on hers, and damned if they weren't sympathetic.

"Don't go yet," Kiley said.

Kendra stopped, but didn't turn back around. She couldn't really. Dax's eyes had latched onto hers somehow and there was a conversation happening between them that went something like,

Dax: It's gonna be okay. I'm here for you.

Kendra: I will punch you in the face if you feel sorry for me.

Dax: I'll feel sorry for you anyway, though.

"The baby's not here yet," Kiley went on, coming up behind her, touching her shoulder with a hand that landed like a nervous bird ready to take flight if she so much as twitched. "And there's plenty of time before she does. And I really want you to stay."

"Why?"

"Because I miss you," she said. And it sounded honest and kind of sad. And since, allegedly, her sister didn't believe in conning people anymore, it probably was. Besides, Kendra always knew when Kiley was lying.

Kendra turned to face her twin. Kiley's skin was like a

blushing peach, and her eyes shone with a glimmering coat of unshed tears.

"I'm not gonna let you tell me how to be."

"Maybe we don't have to talk about that right now," Kiley said.

Kendra rolled her eyes. "What *are* we gonna talk about?"

"Holiday Ranch. Married life. The fact that I can no longer tie my own shoes." She bent slightly forward, reaching down with both arms to demonstrate. Her fingertips only made it to her knees.

Kendra tried not to laugh, but it burst through anyway, as involuntary as a sneeze.

Kiley smiled too. "I'm gonna name her after Mom."

"Ah hell, just keep pouring on the mush, why don't you?" Kendra blinked wet heat from her eyes. "I don't like being judged," she said. "You don't get to do that to me, Kiley."

Kiley lowered her head. Her husband Rob, who'd been standing quietly a few steps behind her, came closer, leaned in, whispered in her ear.

She blew like an agitated mare and met Kendra's eyes again. "Okay," she said. "Come on, let me show you what I've been up to around here."

Sighing, Kendra nodded. To her surprise, Dax fell into step beside her as she followed Kiley and Rob up a pretty stone footpath toward the barns. Leaning sideways, he whispered, "I'm sorry I didn't warn you she was pregnant."

"Why didn't you?" Kendra was really pissed about that.

"Because it was between two sisters. If there's one thing I've learned from Rob and his family, it's that a man has to be damn near suicidal to meddle in a mess between sisters."

"So it wasn't a little bit of payback for what I did to you before?" She looked up at him as she asked the question.

He seemed surprised. "Not even a little bit," he said. "I'm not wired that way, Kendra. I'm not vindictive. You know me better than that."

He was hurt she'd even asked. Well, hell, she was killing it here, wasn't she? "You're right," she said. "I do know you better than that."

He gave a nod and started walking again.

Sighing, Kendra did, too.

She knew what her sister was doing. Kiley probably figured if Kendra spent some time here in this goodie-two-shoes town with her husband's goodie-two-shoes family, she'd see the light, throw away her entire life, and join the goodie-two-shoes movement. It was a stupid plan, and a wasted effort, since she hadn't run a con in a year and a half.

Until now. She was here for one reason and one reason only. To save her father's life.

CHAPTER THREE

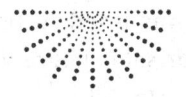

Dax couldn't take his eyes off Kendra. Kiley led them all around the place, moving in a kind of waddle that made you just want to hug her. And then maybe carry her the rest of the way. It was a heavy load she was hauling, and she was a little thing. He didn't know how women did it, to be honest. Rob stayed close by, and he was watchful, careful, opening doors, pointing out hazards she might trip over, hovering near enough to catch her should she stumble. It was obvious that Kiley was both irritated and touched by the attention.

Kendra was pretty well focused on the place, though. And no wonder. It was where she'd spent her childhood, and very different now from the last time she'd seen it. The larger barn had been refitted with stables that lined both sides. The horses were outside grazing, but the place still smelled like them, and their molasses flavored grain and good straw bedding. He loved the smell of a stable.

Kendra seemed to like it, too. He noticed her inhaling nasally, closing her eyes for a second. She had the ability to savor life like no one he'd ever known, in those rare moments when she could get out of her head long enough. Sadly, she didn't do that very often.

When she opened her eyes again, she caught him looking and plastered an unimpressed expression on her face.

They walked through, then out the other end and back around to the smaller barn, which had been completely converted, too. One part was sectioned off, and had a counter with a cash register. It was lined in pegged wallboards, every inch covered in items for sale. There were spinning racks and display shelves of all sorts. The merchandise changed with the seasons and ranged widely in value. In the summer, there'd been sparklers and full-sized flags and kits to hang them. Up to a couple of weeks ago, there'd been Jack-o-lantern carving kits with fancy patterns, all sorts of Halloween decorations, and a rack of costumes ten feet long. But Halloween had passed, and now the shop was filled with wreaths of orange and yellow maple leaves, and cornucopia shells, some filled to overflowing and some empty so you could fill them yourself. Lots of turkeys, lots of native Americans sitting down to feast with the newly arrived immigrant pilgrims.

"This is really... this is *nice*, Kiley," Kendra said, and it was sincere. She moved through the shop, picking up a Thanksgiving-themed apron. It was white with russet piping, and had a bountiful table stitched together in a mosaic of different colored cloth, and quilted onto the front. The word "Grateful" was embroidered above it.

"Wow," she said. She checked out the tiny, tight stitches and then the price tag. "Are you kidding me? Is this with a markup, Kiley?"

"Twenty-five percent," Kiley said.

"Where did you find something this good for this price?"

"The town librarian makes them. Velma Scruggs, you remember her?"

"Velma is still the librarian?" Kendra met her sister's eyes and smiled.

Dax stopped breathing. It was genuine, that smile. There was no calculation behind it, no motive. It was bubbling out from underneath the mask she wore. It looked the same, that mask. But it wasn't real.

The real thing was almost blinding. And Dax knew the difference better than anyone else, except maybe Kiley.

"We turned the whole second level into a haunted house for September and October," Kiley said, her pride and excitement in the bright resonance of her voice. "I swear, every kid in town went through ten times."

"What did you charge them?"

"Not enough that you wouldn't tell me to charge more," she said. "I felt bad for the kids who came back over and over and just stopped charging them at all."

Kendra lifted her brows. "You running a business or a non-profit?"

"We did fine," Kiley said.

"Sure. Next year, sell season passes. Charge as little as you want, but getting something out of every visit is better than getting nothing out of some of them." She looked around. "And get a handful of vending machines out here. Pop, snacks. You have teenagers, you're gonna need snacks. Get machines instead of hiring staff to feed 'em, and you're immediately making more money without doing another thing."

Kiley shot her husband an unspoken question. He replied with his eyes somehow. Dax saw the communication happening, but it was entirely private. That was amazing. Was every couple in love like that?

Kiley turned back to Kendra and said, "That's a really good idea."

"Of course it is. Knowing what people want and how to give it to them is the first lesson Jack ever taught us." Something flashed in her eyes when she said her father's name. Dax saw it and frowned and felt like the guy whose job it was to watch the skies, waiting for signs of alien life. Nothing, nothing, nothing, then suddenly something. And before you can even figure out what it was, you're back to staring at nothing again and wondering if the something was anything at all.

He would hate that job.

He hated the job he was facing right then, too. Caleb Montgomery, a local lawyer and Rob's step-brother-in-law, had got him the name of an extremely discreet accountant. The fellow was already going over the track's books.

Dax had to protect his mother from any legal fallout from his father's behavior. So he couldn't let the SRA anywhere *near* those books until he knew what was in them, and figured out how to protect his mother from being prosecuted for it. She'd been a silent partner, just collecting a check for her share every quarter, but Cal had assured him if anything illegal had gone on at the track, she would face charges anyway.

The lawyers were waiting for him to get back to them, to accept or refuse his inheritance. He needed to stall them and wasn't sure he could.

The crew was heading back toward the house now. They'd asked Kendra to stay for lunch, and they'd included him in the invitation. So he headed to the house with the rest of them, and watched Kendra's eyes as they walked through the kitchen with its rustic white cabinets and wrought-iron hardware, and its red and white checkerboard tiled backsplash and white granite countertop. He watched her as they went into the big, cozy living room with the sectional sofa all draped in shaggy, fringy, snuggly looking throws in brown and tan and burgundy and mustard. Throw pillows in the same shades, but not too many. And not those square, rock hard ones either. These were soft, made for resting your head on.

He'd rested his head on them more than once when he'd still

been drinking. Right after Kendra left town sixteen months ago and three days ago. Not an excuse, just a fact.

Rob said, "I'm gonna order pizza. Any requests?"

"Ham and pineapple," both twins said at once.

"And some wings on the side," Kiley said. "And tell 'em not to be stingy with the blue cheese."

Kendra grinned, but snapped her mouth straight again.

Rob texted in the pizza order, then inclined his head toward the kitchen and Dax followed him out there. Rob poured tea from a glass pitcher shaped a lot like his wife, over ice in tall glasses. After he'd closed the fridge, he handed a glass to Dax.

"I'm gonna ask you a favor," he said. "And it's a big one."

"And it has to do with Kendra," Dax replied as his hand closed around the cold, dewy glass.

"Yeah."

"I ever mention that my sponsor thinks I need to avoid her the way I avoid alcohol?"

"If there's any chance this would push you off the wagon, Dax—"

"You don't get pushed off the wagon, and you don't fall off it either. You jump. It's a choice, and it's one I don't intend on making." He hadn't had a drink since last December, and he was kind of excited about that first anniversary. "What do you want me to do?"

"Keep an eye on Kendra, that's all."

"Why not say what you really mean, Rob? You want me to pretend I'm into her again, and get close enough to find out what she's up to."

Rob made an exaggerated frown. "I'd never ask you to do anything dishonest. You know me better than that."

It was true, Rob was probably the most honest man in town.

"But I think we both know you wouldn't be pretending."

"That's a low blow, Rob."

Rob nodded. "I don't know why she's here. Why now, with

the baby due any time? And could it have anything to do with her father?"

"What would it have to do with him?" Dax asked.

Rob said, "She messed up his plan to swindle a half million from the townsfolk of Big Falls. Made her a local hero to them. Made her an enemy to him. And he's not a nice man."

"I don't think even Jack Kellogg would hurt his own daughter," Dax said. "And even if he did, there's no way Kendra would help." He took a long drink from the tall, dewy glass, then shook his head. "She might be bad to the bone, Rob, but she loves her sister."

"But we both know Kiley isn't why she's here. Don't we?"

Dax sighed. "I'm not gonna lie to her." Then he shrugged. "But you're right. I won't have to. Truth is, I'm as curious as you are about what she's doing back here." He felt the craving for a stiff drink start writhing around in that spot above his stomach but below his ribs. *That's just my most deadly weakness waking up. I'm stronger than a weakness.* And he changed the subject in his mind to the one most likely to distract him, Kendra. He now had a slightly more noble-feeling reason to be around her. Convenient how that ended the inner battle he'd been waging, with part of him telling himself to stay as far away from her as possible, and another part wanting to be with her as much as he could before she floated away again, like a dandelion seed on a summer breeze.

Rob had become his best friend. Kiley could be in danger, and her baby, too. Jack Kellogg was a criminal who'd done serious time in a serious prison. And he was furious with his daughter. The good one.

Kendra had helped Kiley, though. In the end, she'd chosen the right side. Impossible to say whether she'd make the same choice again. She was angry at being kept in the dark about the impending arrival of her niece. The daughter of her twin, which seemed to make it even worse, somehow. He didn't blame her for being pissed about that. But he knew Kendra Kellogg well enough to know, you can never *really know* Kendra Kellogg. Or what she might do if she felt like her back was to the wall.

If he had to walk the razor's edge with Kendra to keep Rob's two girls safe, then that's what he was going to do. Get close to her again, only this time it would be him running a game on her. He was going to find out why she was really in town and what Jack Kellogg knew.

It would be like dancing with a bottle of fine Jim Beam and not taking a sip.

He couldn't take even a little taste of Kendra, or he'd fall into that bottle of her headfirst. And he had a feeling he'd never get back out.

~

Kendra was pacing her corner room, surprised the noise from below was so muffled. Just a dull din, almost a hum. And yet The Long Branch was packed, mostly with tourists. It was after nine p.m. and the activity was on the upswing. More and more sets of headlights slowed and angled as cars filled the parking lot. Business must be booming.

Her room was at a back corner, so the headlights didn't glare straight through into her eyes. She only saw them when gazing out the window.

Someone had redone the guest rooms since she'd been here last. They used to be plain bordering on Spartan. But this one, at least, was all dressed up in an old-time theme that fit with the old west motif downstairs. There were hurricane lamps and bed curtains, a washstand with an antique bowl and pitcher made of white porcelain with pink roses and gold edging, all spider-webbed with age. The wallpaper had roses too, vertical rows of them. Cream colored curtains hung in four windows with pink satin tiebacks hooked around brass holders. Each holder had a round inset, white ceramic with pink roses. Behind the curtains, there were window shades with lace edges, their color meant to look age-yellowed.

Portraits of times gone by graced the walls in antique frames with thick but spotless glass. Black and white prints, enlarged from the original tin types. A man with a moustache that drooped lower than his chin and solemn eyes. A cowboy posing beside his painted pony. His face was a stone mountain range, his scowl-for-the-camera, given away by the dimple pulling at one cheek.

It was a busy room. She'd like it a lot better with the lights off.

What was she going to do? Dax was fighting her too hard. Yes, he'd come along with her to Kiley's place, but reluctantly, and he'd been keeping a minimum of three feet of space between them at all times. Sure, she'd win him over eventually, but she didn't have that kind of time.

She stopped pacing and looked at the bed. Modern comforter, white with roses. If she had to look at one more rose, she'd puke. She yanked the comforter off the bed, wadded it up, and hurled it into a corner with a growl that sounded vaguely like *gruck groses!*

Knock knock knock. "You okay in there?" Dax called.

"It's open."

The knob turned, door opened. He stuck his head through and looked around. "You got a bear in here with you?"

She grinned. Then she laughed. He'd pulled the plug, and her frustration was draining away. "No bear."

He came the rest of the way in, closed the door behind him, and looked around. "Wow. I'm really glad this isn't the room they let me dry out in after my last bender."

"You had a bender?"

He nodded. "I'd been drinking way too much for way too

long. And I knew it. I was riding a train off a cliff and didn't have the brains to get off before it went over. And then it did."

She lowered her head. "After what I did to you."

"A drunk can always find a reason to drink. You were mine, but if you hadn't been, something else would have, sooner or later."

"I'm sorry, you know. I never felt bad about a mark before, but you... I'd undo it if I could. But that would mean we'd never have had that time together."

He lowered his head, not looking into her eyes. "That time together was you running a con."

She nodded. "It was also the best time of my life." She held up both hands when he shot her a look that was almost accusing. "No game. That's the truth. I regret taking that money from you. I really do."

He lowered his head. "Yeah, well, I'm not blameless. I mean, come on, a kidney transplant? Out of the blue like that? I wanted to believe you, even when I knew better. I knew when I handed you that cash. On some level, I knew."

"You can't take the blame for what I did."

"I can at least admit that I was a willing participant."

"So..." They were playing tag with their eyes and she was it. "Are you saying I'm forgiven?"

"Ninety-nine percent forgiven. I'm holding back a point for when you pay it back."

She blinked and pulled in her chin. "You think I'm gonna pay it back?"

"I think it's the right thing to do."

"Uh-uh. No way. You just stood there and took the blame for being conned."

"*You* said—" he countered, but she held up a hand.

"Fifty percent. I'm half to blame, you're half to blame. Chalk your half up to a learning experience. I'll pay you back my half. Eventually." She turned her hand sideways. "Deal?"

"I like you when you're being your legitimate self, you know that?"

She thrust her hand at him. "Deal?"

"Deal." His hand enveloped hers completely in warmth and restrained power. She'd always loved Dax Russell's big strong hands.

He closed his eyes, took a breath, and let go.

"So... now what?" she asked.

He looked at her, then at the bed. "I um...I don't..."

"Not *that kind* of now what. I meant, why are you here, in my room?"

"Oh, right." He smiled in what looked like real relief and said, "I thought you might want to see The Twig."

She glanced at his zipper and said, "Is that what you're calling it these days?" He was blushing before she gave him a wink to let him know she was kidding. "I knew what you meant. And yes, I'm *dying* to see what Joey's got going out there."

Fifteen minutes later, they were standing beside a carbon copy of The Long Branch, about a third the size of the original. Its overhead sign spelled out "The Twig" in the same western font. Dax opened a metal panel on the outside wall, flipped a lever, and the place lit up like Christmas, inside and out. Tall lights on poles aimed down from above, and he took her hand like it was an ordinary thing to do and tugged her a few trotting steps away from the building.

"Mini-golf course," he said, pointing. The obstacles were bucking broncos and bad guys, saloon doors and a jailbreak scene. Everything cowboy.

She barely had time to see all that before he led her around to the back of the building, pointing out a wide area that looked like a ghost town. There were one-dimensional store fronts with fake broken windows and missing doors, broken fences, empty watering troughs, square bales of hay stacked here and there.

"Paintball course," he told her. Then he kept going around to the right of the building, on the side nearest The Long Branch. It was a worn patch of dirt with a wide path winding around it. "Racetrack. There's a fleet of little electric cars." He pointed and she spotted eight mini-cars parked along one side of the track inside a locked paddock.

"Did you help Joey plan the racetrack?" she asked.

"No, no, he came up with it all himself. He and Emily. You have her to thank for all the roses in your room by the way. She's very into decorating and themes."

"Oh. Yeah, it's uh…a lot of roses."

"It is. She did a few rooms cowboy themed. They're not as bad."

He pulled out a keyring and started to unlock the door. She said, "I only asked if you planned the racetrack because of your years working at one. The one your father owns. Or owned, I guess."

He paused in unlocking the door, blinked twice, then swallowed hard, finished unlocking it, and swung it open. "The big room on the left here," he leaned in, flipped a light switch. "contains the ball pit and bounce house." She looked past him, gave a nod. He turned that light off and moved on. "The whole back of the building is an arcade." Again, he leaned in and flipped the light switch. Rows and rows of arcade games five deep and four wide, took up every bit of available space. He shut the light off. The room they were in held a service counter, and the space behind it, a walk-in cooler.

"This is where you rent your equipment for the games, buy tokens for the arcade, and get soft drinks and snacks, including soft-serve ice cream. Dips and sprinkles are extra."

She nodded her approval. "Nobody spends money like a parent," she said. "This is gonna be a goldmine. Hell, between what Joe's doing here and Holiday Ranch, Big Falls is going to start being a destination for low-key, kid-friendly fun."

"Not to mention the birthday party business," Dax said. "Joey put a lot into it, but I think it'll pay off, if he figured out how to promote it properly."

She nodded, and this time as they went back outside, him turning off lights on the way, she took hold of his hand as he locked the door behind them. "Seems like Joey's found his calling," she said softly. "Kiley and Rob, too." She tugged him around the building, found the control panel, turned the lever off, and closed the lid. "What about you?"

"What *about* me?"

"Have you found your calling?"

"Working with horses. Training them. That's what I love doing best."

"And what about the track? Your dad's business. It's yours now, isn't it?" She searched his face as he stood there, stone silent. Then she widened her eyes and said, "He didn't disinherit you, did he? Because of me?"

So her visit wasn't about Kiley at all. It was about the track and the fortune that came with it. Dax stood there, trying to work out the best answer, but it was impossible, because he was reeling. He shouldn't be. He knew her. He'd figured she was here for a reason. He'd just been hoping he was wrong.

"I'm sorry. I didn't mean to pry."

He'd believed the emotion in her eyes when she'd been with her sister, and the empathy in them when she talked about his father's death. But her mention of the track just blew the cover off her lies.

In a kneejerk reaction, he decided to repay deception with deception and said, "Yes. He disinherited me."

She frowned as if that didn't quite compute, and then plastered on a look of sympathy. "I'm so sorry, Dax."

"I'm not. I don't mind at all. I like my life just fine." And he did. And he figured that probably answered the question that had been plaguing him ever since he'd watched his old man die.

What to do about the inheritance. Now he knew. He'd meant what he'd said. He didn't want it, and it was a load off his mind to know that for sure. He still couldn't refuse it until he'd found whatever surprises were hiding in the books and figured out a way to protect his mother from the repercussions of them. But at least he knew for sure that he didn't want it.

She lowered her head. He thought he saw disappointment in her eyes, but she was so good at hiding her feelings that he didn't get a long enough glimpse of it to be sure. When she lifted it again, her eyes were bright and her smile was counterfeit. She changed the subject with ease. "It's odd being back home again. My sister being a pillar of the community now. Me, too, by extension. That's just…it's weird."

"I meant to ask about that. You're using your own name now. Last time you were here, you were pretending to be dead."

"Oh, that. Yeah, that's all cleared up."

"Cleared up? They made faking your own death legal, and I missed the memo?"

She nodded. "Dad convinced the cop on the case that it was an accident. That I'd run away from the halfway house before the fire and wasn't aware one of the bodies had been identified as my own."

"And the cop believed it?"

"No, but Dad also had photos of him in some pretty compromising positions with a whore, so…" She shrugged.

God, that family of hers.

"Kiley said that if you were pretending to be dead, you must have had a good reason. She suspected someone dangerous was after you."

She shrugged. "Mmm."

"Mmm? What kind of an answer is that?"

She shrugged. "I dated a guy who turned all stalker on me, and I got scared. Whatever, it's history now. You know what I'd like? I'd like to go riding. Here I am in Big Falls with a brother-in-law who has a whole herd of horses and a...friend...who's an expert trainer. I almost *have to* go riding, don't I?"

"You almost have to," he agreed.

"Will you take me?" She tipped her head up and made her eyes as Disney princess as possible.

His internal reaction was to go warm and gooey. His brain was the only part of him still onto her lies. "You really want me to take you riding, even now that you know I'm not gonna inherit a nickel?"

Her smile died. Her eyes turned wounded. "I guess I deserved that." She looked at the ground. "I'm sure Rob will take me if I ask." Heaving a gigantic sigh, she started back toward The Long Branch. "Thanks for showing me this. I'll see you around."

She walked away.

And he let her go.

For about a hundred steps. He counted them. And then he ran to catch up to her and said, "I'm heading out to the ranch anyway in the morning. Come out around eight?"

Her smile was as bright as a supernova. "I can't wait."

CHAPTER FOUR

As she stood in the fragrant stable watching hay dust dance in a beam of morning sunlight, Dax saddled a pair of horses for them. Kendra still couldn't believe it. Sweet, kind, loyal, honest Dax Russell was lying to her.

Lying.

To *her.*

He was his father's heir.

Nealand Russel had only died a couple of days ago, though. They'd just had the funeral day before yesterday. Dax had attended with his mother, and taken the next flight home. Kendra wasn't supposed to know those things, but she did. The will probably hadn't even been looked at yet by anyone other than the lawyers, who'd probably torn into it before the old man finished his final breath. Greedy bastards. She hated lawyers.

Well, except for Caleb Montgomery, on Main Street. He was country, through and through. Could've had a future in politics, if he could've stomached it. She imagined he was too honest for it, though. He was one of the good guys. They were a rare breed, but Texas and Oklahoma seemed to produce more than their share. They were the boys who grew up around cattle and crops. Even if their daddies weren't ranchers or farmers, those were the summer jobs they took all through high school. They liked cars, country music, fishing, and they didn't mind fighting when it was called for.

Dax was like that. Born and raised in Tennessee, another state with a bumper crop of good guys. He'd told her all about it one night when they'd had too many beers together, and wound up snuggled on her sofa back in Aurora Springs, NY. She'd been there with Jack, scoping out the rich widows who frequented the horse races wearing big brimmed hats and sucking down mint juleps and pretending they were in Kentucky instead of a little town in New York. The whole place looked as if it had been teleported from the 1890s. The houses. The shops. Jack had also been scoping out connections. Horseracing drew bosses like horseshit drew flies.

That was where she and Jack had met Vester Caine, the "business man" responsible for most of the heroin in the northeast. Jack said he was a lucrative connection to have. Kendra disagreed. She'd pegged him as evil right from the start. If that bastard hurt her father....

She shifted her thoughts deliberately back to Dax, wondering why he'd lied to her.

Dax had told her one night long ago, something she'd already known. That his father had inherited Aurora Downs from his grandfather. And how all the other nearby tracks were owned by the State Racing Association. All but Aurora Downs. The SRA had taken them all over decades ago, to get rid of the organized crime elements that had infiltrated so many of them. But one of Dax's ancestors had pull with somebody important, and a grandfather clause had been created. The clause allowed family-owned tracks to remain family-owned, so long as there was an heir to inherit them. And at the time, Aurora Downs had been the only family-owned track left.

If Dax's family ran out of heirs, the track would go to the SRA. It could never be sold.

Dax's family had moved from Tennessee to New York once his father inherited the track, and he'd spent his teen years working there. He didn't have any siblings. His parents had divorced. There was no one else to inherit. The track was either going to him or to the SRA.

Dax had lied to her. His old man didn't have a choice but to leave him that track.

So his offer to take her riding might not be something to celebrate after all. What if he was up to something?

What if he knew she was?

"All set," Dax said, giving a final tug on the cinch.

She turned to look at him, at his sweet smile and big blue eyes. He had the kind of face that made you think there ought to be trumpets announcing his arrival every time he came around. The kind of face that would soothe the most inconsolable shrieking infant, or the most obnoxious adult. She loved his face. It wasn't the face of a con-man or a liar. He didn't have a dishonest bone in his big beautiful body.

He smiled at her and rubbed his thumb over an imaginary smudge on his cheek. "What? Have I got something on my face?"

"Yeah. There's handsome smeared all over it." He wasn't up to anything. Not her Dax. Never, not in a million years. Maybe he really believed he'd been disinherited. Maybe he didn't know better because lawyers were slow and next week was Thanksgiving.

He dropped to one knee, patting the other. "Step on up."

"You know I've never ridden a horse in my life, right?"

"Yes, I do know that. You've told me five times this morning. You seem to keep forgetting this was your idea." He patted his thigh again. "Step on up."

She put her hands on his shoulders and one foot on his thigh.

"That's right. Now, grab onto the pommel instead of my shoulders, and swing your leg over. And don't worry, I'm not gonna let you fall."

She didn't. She put her foot back on the floor and looked at the dark brown mare with the super-model mane. Patting the horse's neck, she said, "I feel like I should introduce myself before presuming to climb all up on your back." The mare turned and gazed back at her with huge brown eyes that wanted to suck all the badness right out of her soul. "Hi," she said. "I'm Kendra."

The horse replied with a soft nicker. Then she faced front again and gave that mane a shake. Kendra sent Dax a look, eyebrows raised. "I think she just said, 'don't hate me because I'm beautiful.'"

Dax laughed. "She said her name's Sweet Caroline, and she's happy to have you onboard."

"So she's a flight attendant?"

"Up you go." He grabbed her butt and lifted. "Swing your leg over."

It was a shame she'd stopped understanding English the second his big hands closed over her cheeks. His touch sent heat and memory sizzling through her whole body and she froze, every bit of her focused on feeling it. Relishing it.

It had been a long time. She still wanted him. She didn't think that part of it had ever really ended. It had been so good, the sex between them. Long, lazy nights of slow, tender lovemaking. Steamy interludes of passionate pleasure. The touches. The looks. When they'd been together everything had been intimate between them. Even mundane things.

"Swing your leg over," he said, bending to speak close, his breath warm on her ear, and neck. She shivered and closed her eyes. "Kendra?"

"Oh, uh, yeah." She only spoke troglodyte now, but it was better than nothing. She pulled herself up and swung her leg over, moving her butt, regrettably, out of his delicious hands and onto a much harder and less fun saddle. Her heart was beating fast as she looked down at him.

He met her eyes, frowned a little. Sure, he saw it all. "You're blushing like a sunburn," he said, "It's not like that's the first time I've had your backside in my hands, Kendra Lee."

"That's the problem, Dax Beauregard."

He winced and sucked air through his teeth. "You're one of only two people alive who know my middle name. Let's keep it that way." He handed her the reins, closing her hand around them just so, and placed her other hand on the pommel. And then he left his hand on top of hers for a few extra beats, and she swore she felt it tighten a little, and maybe his fingers moved in the most subtle, most minuscule caress.

He cleared his throat, took his hand away. "Use the pommel for grip and balance, never the reins. They are only for communicating with the horse, not to keep yourself from falling off. Okay?"

"Got it."

He checked to be sure both her feet were securely in the stirrups, made a few adjustments to get them just the right length, and finally turned and got on his own horse, a mottled dark gray mare that turned blue when they rode outside and the slanting sunlight fell on her coat. She had a vivid black mane and tail.

"Who's the other person," she asked. "Who knows your middle name?"

"My mother," he said.

"Caroline." Then she frowned. "Is this horse I'm riding named after your mother, Dax?"

"You remember my mom's name?"

She lowered her eyes, and clamped her legs tighter when the

horse gave a harmless hop. When she was sure she wasn't going to fall off, she said, "Your mother is kind of unforgettable," she said. "But even if I'd never met her, I'd remember. I think I remember everything you ever told me." She used to love the way he would talk to her, back when he thought she was real. Back when he thought she was good. He'd tell her things about his childhood, about his life, about things that mattered to him.

That was when she'd started to change, that time with him. He was so good it was contagious. Typhoid Dax. He'd infected her. She'd been losing her edge since the day she first met him, waiting tables in a joint where high-end people came for lunch. Track owners and gamblers, breeders and fans. Poor people don't go to horse races. They're too smart to throw money away watching horses run. They'd rather see them gallop across a meadow, or ride them across one, like she was doing right then. This was nice.

"I've had that mare since I was nineteen," he said. "She was boarding at Mom's place in New York. I just got her moved down here this past summer. Rob insisted."

She nodded. His mother owned a small boarding stable near his father's racetrack.

There were other horses in the meadow, soaking up the autumn sunshine and nibbling on grass and wildflowers. She and Dax took a trail that followed the fence line, riding past spindly legged colts, who stuck so close to their mammas, Kendra was afraid they'd get stepped on.

It was quiet. Quiet tended to make her uncomfortable. She said, "If I'm riding your horse, who are you riding?"

"This is Louise."

"That's my sister's middle name."

"Rob thought naming her Kiley would get confusing," he said. "She's a blue roan. A stunner, isn't she?"

"She is." Her horse jumped over something in the path, and the landing knocked her whole body dangerously sideways. She almost jerked the reins to hold herself upright, but caught the impulse just in time, gripped the pommel, squeezed her thighs, and got herself right again.

"Nice," he said.

She found herself beaming with pride that she hadn't fallen off a horse. Big fat hairy deal. She wanted to talk to him some more. She wanted to talk to him about the track and his inheritance and try to find out why he'd lied to her about it.

But he looked at her with that serene smile and said, "You're not here. Stop all that chatter going on in your pretty head, and try to just be right here."

She frowned at him. "I don't know how to do that," she said, and it was completely honest.

He said, "Listen. Try and count how many different sounds you can hear."

Kendra listened. The first sound she noticed was the steady rhythmic plodding of the horses' hooves over the packed earth trail. It was a soft sound, a *gentle thud, tha-thud, tha-thud, tha-thud*. She noticed that her hips rocked in the saddle right in time with the beat, if she let them, and tried to relax her stiff posture a little more. That was one of a hundred tips Dax had given while he'd been saddling the horses, relax your hips and rock.

She could hear the Cimarron, too. The river unwound not a hundred feet from the trail, to the right. There was splashing and gurgling where it tumbled over rocks and fallen limbs, but behind and beneath that, a deeper, constant murmur of raw power.

There were birds singing, too. A loud one repeated the same cry over and over, and then as she paid attention, she heard others. Warblers warbled and songbirds sang. She listened even harder, leaning slightly forward in her saddle, eyes intense. There was a bumble bee buzzing from flower to flower somewhere.

"Works better if you don't try too hard," Dax said. "Just relax and let the sounds come to you. Same as the smells."

She could only smell horse. But no, there were late-blooming lilies that pulled her gaze right to them as soon as her nose caught a whiff. The river had a scent of its own, and so did the trees and even, she thought, the sunshine.

And Dax. He smelled clean and familiar and good.

He wasn't up to anything. He'd asked her to come riding because he still cared about her. And he'd probably lied about his inheritance so he could assure himself she wasn't going to try to con him out of it.

Yeah, that was probably it.

She relaxed even more, kind of sinking into her own body from a posture that had been tense and tight. She didn't even realize how tense and tight until she let go of it. She rode along on Sweet Caroline and smelled horse and leather and flowers and Dax, and she listened to the songs and buzzes and splashes and hoof steps that came from everywhere and everything.

It was the most peaceful morning she thought she had ever spent.

∽

After their ride, Kiley invited Kendra to go baby shopping. Dax didn't expect her to agree, once she found out three other women were also going along; Rob's cousin Sophie, sister-in-law Emily, and Allie Wakeland, who was three weeks less pregnant than Kiley. She was also the talk of Big Falls because she didn't have so much as a boyfriend, and because when her war-hero brother got back from Afghanistan, he was going to hunt down whoever had got her pregnant, and murder him.

To Dax's stunned surprise, Kendra accepted the invitation, and went off for a girls' day out that was completely not her kind of thing.

He and Rob were working with the oldest colts that day. In Dax's opinion, the most important part of training was the relationship between horse and trainer, and you couldn't start building that too soon. They spent a lot of time with the colts, touched them frequently, and worked on keeping their attention rapt even when distractions, from passing cars to bumblebees, came along.

Rob said, "She's too close to her due date to be running around shopping malls. I don't even know how her little legs can *carry* all that around a shopping mall."

Dax, who'd been waiting for a break in Rob's over-protective, dad-to-be griping, so he could change the subject entirely, said, "Sophie's a doctor, Emily's a vet, and Allie's almost as far along as Kiley is. I'm pretty sure your wife is safer in a mall with those three than she would be in her own living room. Besides, Kendra's with her."

"Yeah," he said with a weighty look. Then he sighed. "It's scary, that's all. I don't like being more than a few yards away from her these days."

"And she hasn't skinned you yet?"

Rob blinked as if Dax was speaking a new language, and then something dawned on his face. "Am I hovering?"

"Hovering. Maybe smothering. Who am I to say? But I do know that women have babies every day without any help at all from the daddies. Aside from that fun part in the beginning." He tried a friendly grin, in case the truth hurt.

Rob sighed. "You're right. I'm acting like a crazy man."

"That's the thing about crazy—you can't see it when you're in it." He shrugged. "I might be close to slipping into a whole other kind of crazy, myself."

Rob looked away from the colt he'd been brushing, a still spindly brown fellow with a mane just at that spikey stage that made him look like a punk rocker. His eyes were wide and worried. Rob's, not the colt's. "Kendra?"

Dax nodded. "For what it's worth, I'm sure her coming here had nothing to do with Kiley. She was legitimately shocked to find out about the baby."

"Then why is she here?" Fireball, named for his resemblance to the *Rudolf* character, craned his neck around and nickered. *More, please.*

"I'm not sure yet, but she knows about my father, and has been asking about the track. Whether he left it to me. And uh... I've got reason to think there's something going on with the books there."

Rob shot him a worried look. "What do you mean, 'something going on with the books?' Are you okay here, Dax?"

"*I'm* okay. I'm not an owner. But my mother is. Rob, this has to stay between us. I trust you."

"You can trust me absolutely. You're my friend, Dax." He grinned. "Even if you did kick my ass when we first met."

"Hey, you held your own. Don't sell yourself short. You put a hurtin' on me, too."

"And that's how good a friend you are," Rob said, clapping him on the shoulder. "Letting me believe that."

They shared a laugh, and it died gradually. Dax took a deep breath, and then he went on. "My father's dying words warned me that letting the track go puts my mother at risk. He said she'd go to prison. Something about the books."

"Holy.... What are you gonna do?"

"If I inherit, I'm culpable. If I refuse, my half goes to the SRA, they go over the books, Mom goes to prison."

"This is rough, Dax." Rob rubbed the back of his neck with one hand.

"I've got someone going over the books on the sly. Mom gave me access, though I didn't tell her why I needed it."

Rob nodded. "That's a start. You'll know where you stand." Then he blinked. "You said Kendra was asking about the track. You don't think she's...mixed up in all this, do you?"

He didn't want to think it. "It would be a pretty big coincidence, otherwise," he said. "But even if she's not tangled up in my father's crimes, I imagine she's got some kind of plan to get her fingers into the Aurora Downs pie. She's up to something. She's *always* up to something."

"Ah, hell, Dax. I'm sorry."

He shrugged. "Nothing to be sorry about. I'm gonna get to the bottom of this. It's just hard, being around her and not...." He didn't finish. He didn't have to. Rob had tried pretty hard not to fall for Kendra's twin. He must know exactly what Dax was going through.

"Is there anything I can do?" Rob asked.

Dax shrugged. "I told her Dad didn't leave me a nickel and I wouldn't have taken it even if he had. She's still here. Maybe...."

"Maybe because she knows it's bullshit? Don't you think she did her research and knew the truth before she even came here, especially if the track is *why* she came here?"

"It's not bullshit. I don't want it. She knows that now, so even if that *is* why she came, maybe it's not why she's still here."

He shrugged. "And why do you think she's still here?"

Dax lowered his head. "Not for me. I don't think that. I'm not stupid." Although she *had* seemed near to blissful on that ride with him this morning. She'd seemed different. She'd seemed real. And she'd seemed to be enjoying his company as much as he'd been enjoying hers.

This was dangerous ground he was walking. Skipping. Throwing daisies. She was up to no good. Why couldn't he keep that clear in his brain?

"Maybe she's staying for the baby," Rob said, giving him false hope. "The holidays are coming and she and Kiley—they need each other, you know?"

"If the track is why she came, that's why she came," Dax said. "We at least have to consider she might be staying for the right reasons."

Rob said, "Are you trying to talk yourself into something here?"

He was, he realized. He was trying to convince himself that being with Kendra while at the same time trying to find out what she was up to, wasn't the worst idea in the history of bad ideas. When he knew damn well it was.

But he had a reason for shining Kendra on a little. He had to protect his mother. He couldn't let her be prosecuted for his father's crimes and he had to find out whether Kendra was tangled up with those crimes.

Maybe he could keep his heart out of it. Maybe...for a little while.

And then the memory replayed in his mind, of her riding beside him along the tree-lined trail, sunlight dappling her silvery blond hair. She'd smiled over at him, eyes sparkling a reflection of the sheer pleasure she was feeling, and he wondered if he was lying to himself.

~

Kendra was not intimidated by the leading ladies of Big Falls. Doc Sophie, cousin to the McIntyre fortune and married to CMA winning singer songwriter Darryl Champlain. Emily, the veterinarian married to Joey and the McIntyre fortune, The Long Branch Saloon, and the adorable "Twig" currently sprouting behind it. And 8 month's pregnant Allie Wakeland, photographer from a military family who were local heroes. Her brother was serving now. Her brother-in-law had made the ultimate sacrifice a year ago. There was a monument to him in the park.

Then there was her sister, Kiley, savior of Big Falls, who'd stopped a con man from leaving town with the half mil he'd swindled out of them summer before last. They overlooked the fact that said con man was her dad, and probably didn't even know that Kendra had helped her pull it off.

Saved her is more like it. Jack was about to catch on when I pulled Kiley's ass out of the fire.

She wasn't intimidated.

The hell she wasn't. They were four Cinderellas and a wicked stepsister. Only not step. Twin. A wicked twinsister.

They walked through the Mall of Tucker Lake together. Kendra told herself that she was also a highly accomplished woman. She was one of the best cons in the biz. And while she'd taken a break from running games on people, she hadn't really given it up. She'd been running promotions for small businesses online for the past year. At first, as an assistant to an indie marketer, and then hanging up an online shingle of her own. As it turned out, convincing consumers to buy something was what she'd been doing all her life. Now she was doing it legally. And she was making bank.

She wasn't ashamed of either incarnation of her career. Except when it came to Dax.

Dax. The memory of their morning ride returned like a warmed blanket wrapped all around her. He hadn't been able to take his eyes off her. She'd let herself forget how it felt to be that adored by someone.

He was a good man. Probably the best man she'd ever known.

Kiley said, "Oh, restrooms!" and pointed as excitedly as if she'd just crossed the Sahara and spotted a lemonade stand.

"Thank God!" Allie said.

"Go ahead, we'll wait." Emily smiled as she said it.

Kendra didn't know whether to run off with the pair of preggos or stay with the saints. Sophie put a hand on her arm and said, "We'll be right here, Kiley. Take your time." And she winked.

"Uh, yeah," Kendra said with a sideways frown. "We'll be right here."

They wanted to talk to her alone. She braced herself, figuring she was in for it. They were either going to accuse her of something or question her motives, and then she'd have to spend the rest of the day with them pretending it was fine. Would the fun never end?

Kiley and Allie waddled away to the restrooms.

Sophie said, "My God, it took her long enough. She must have a bladder like a camel."

"I'd have had to go three times by now, when I was carrying Matilda Louise," Emily put in.

Kiley looked back over her shoulder before going through the restroom door, gave a wave. Did she look worried? Kendra wondered if she was more concerned about her or about them. Them, she decided. Her sister knew better than to worry about her.

The door swung closed, and Emily said, "Okay, great. Now we have to talk fast, they won't give us much time."

"About what?" Kendra asked, because the redheaded vet was animated and smiling, not dark and menacing.

"The baby shower!" She clapped her hands and her grin got wider.

"We started planning it," Sophie said. She was classy. Elegant without trying to be. "Being the closest relatives here."

"Right," Emily said. "But now that you're here, you're closest. We don't want to step on your toes."

"Not that we're dumping it on you, either." Sophie held up both hands. "But you're her sister. If you want to throw it, then—"

"Wait, wait." Kendra gave her head a shake. "You want me to plan a baby shower?"

They looked at each other, then at her. "*Help* plan one. You are her sister," Emily said.

"Her twin sister," Sophie added. Like she might've forgotten.

Emily nodded hard. "Vidalia's helping, too. And Sunny."

She was mentally identifying those people in her head. Vidalia was Kiley's stepmother-in-law. And Sunny, she was the bakery chick, right?

"They'll be back any minute." Emily shot a nervous look at the restroom door. "We want it to be a surprise. Rob doesn't know, either."

"We should meet to go over what we've done so far and we can just start from there, with you in the lead," Sophie said.

"Oooh-kay. Um, when?"

"My office tomorrow morning, say eight a.m?" Sophie asked.

Eight a.m. Why did everyone around here do everything so early?

"Here they come!" Emily said.

"Here's the address." Emily slipped an appointment card into Kendra's hand so sneakily she wouldn't have been surprised if they got busted by a mall cop for a suspected drug deal.

And then Kiley and Allie were back, smiling and holding their baby bumps.

"Well, where do you want to shop first?" Sophie asked, rubbing her hands together and looking at the mall map.

"I'm gonna need nursing bras," Kiley said.

Kendra's jaw literally dropped. "Oh my God, Sis, we have to get you into Victoria's Secret, STAT. You need something drop-dead sexy to wear after this baby's born."

"As a doctor, I concur," Sophie said. Then she wiggled the most perfect set of eyebrows Kendra had ever seen. "I might just pick out something for myself, as long as we're there anyway."

"My lingerie closet is looking a little mom-like, now that you mention it," Emily said.

Kiley was blushing. "You guys are crazy."

Allie rubbed her baby bump and said, "I haven't felt sexy in so long..." She met Kiley's eyes, lifted her brows and said,

"Well, why not? I could get lucky again someday. You never know."

Kiley looked at each of them, and then she grinned that mischievous grin that hadn't changed since they were kids, spinning in the wildflowers, looking up at the stars. "Let's do it!"

∽

When Dax opened the front door, he found a shopping bag tree, with every branch filled. The muffled plea sounded like, "A li'l hep?"

He started plucking bags, and eventually Kendra sighed and said, "That's good, that's good. Thanks." There were still several clutched in her hands, and dangling from her forearms.

"You go a little bit crazy today?" He wondered where she was getting her money. The car. Everything. Was she running a con on some poor rich slob and using Big Falls as her headquarters?

"This isn't all me. Kiley's gal-gang shops like there's no tomorrow." She came inside, looked around. "Kiley went home with Sophie. Guess she's due for an exam."

"I know, Rob's meeting her there. Asked me to wait for you."

"So...what do we do with all this?" She lifted her laden arms.

"Nursery, would be my best guess," Dax said. He headed through the living room and up the stairs to the bedroom beside Rob and Kiley's.

The window was propped open, a fan aimed outward to clear out the smell of the fresh pink paint that had been put on since he'd been in here last. It was a soft, pretty green with a pink stripe a foot wide around the middle. A white crib fit for a princess stood opposite the window.

He watched Kendra, checking it all out. The bookshelf was already piled with titles. The dresser and changing table were white with rainbows painted on them. Every surface held a toy. There were princess dolls, castles, and unicorns everywhere.

Kendra went to the room's center and stood there, turning in a slow circle. "You...think she went overboard on the princess theme a little bit?" she asked softly.

"If I did, I would never say so."

"Neither would I. Still, it's awfully... girlie, isn't it?"

"A muscle car poster would break it up some," Dax said.

Kendra grinned at him. He grinned back and for just a second, he was stuck there, in a bubble of happy with her.

He cleared his throat, looked away. The bubble popped. He set his bags on the floor near the closet and opened it up. "Lots of hangers in here. Should we?"

She set her bags down beside his and pawed through a few of them, past frilly pink fluffy things until she finally found what she wanted and yanked out the tiniest pair of denim bib overalls he'd ever seen in his life. "I picked these out because Diana's got my DNA, too. She's gonna get dirty, and she's gonna break things."

Hearts, he thought. She was gonna break hearts.

They hung each little item on a hanger, but didn't remove any tags.

"You look all bright and shiny, Kendra. Did you have a good time with the girls?"

"Sure." She averted her eyes, focused on folding footie pajamas so tiny he couldn't believe any human being could fit them. Even a newborn. "I mean, they're nice people, you know that. It's no chore being around nice people like that."

He must've looked at her wrong, because when he did, she added, "For limited periods."

"They seemed to like you." She frowned at him and he nodded at the window. "I saw when they dropped you off. Everyone smiling, waving back all the way down the road."

"You saw us pull in and didn't come help me lug all those bags?"

"By the time I got the door, you were already there. I was

putting some things up in the attic for Rob. Babies take up a lot of room. And you're changing the subject. They liked you, didn't they?"

She took her stack of jammies to the white dresser, opened drawers to see where they belonged. "They only *think* they like me. I make people think they like me, Dax. I grew up learning how and I don't think I can even turn it off anymore. I didn't even try, I swear, they just....."

"They just liked you."

"Apparently, I'm supposed to take over planning the baby shower. Can you even imagine?" She'd found the right drawer, was closing it now.

He wasn't sure how to answer the question. "I guess I don't know enough about baby showers to have an opinion."

"It's a surprise, so don't say anything to Rob. We're having a secret meeting tomorrow at the crack of dawn." She rolled her eyes.

There was a hint of insecurity in them. He spotted it like a hawk spotting a garter snake from on high. She was trying to hide it, but she was nervous about being around the Brand-McIntyre females.

"You know you're just as smart and just as pretty as any of them, don't you?"

"Smarter," she said. "And pretty? Come on, Dax, do you think I give a crap about pretty?" She shrugged. "It's fine. Like I said, they're nice. How did your day go?"

For a second he thought she might really want to know, so he said, "I had a text from my mother. She and the lawyers are coming out here to uh..." he hesitated, but decided to plunge ahead. It felt like the best move. He couldn't trap her without any bait, anyway. And he thought he needed to. He needed to know for sure what her game was, so he could keep his mother as far away from it as possible. And his heart, he had to protect that too. So he said it. "To discuss my father's estate."

She had opened the little closet and was hanging up baby clothes on the tiniest hangers he'd ever seen. But she stopped in mid-motion and spoke without turning to look at him. "I thought you said he cut you out of his will."

"Nope."

"So you just told me that, because...what, you figured if I knew you had the track, I'd try to con you out of it?"

"I don't have the track. I'll never have the track. I don't want it. So while my father didn't disinherit me, I'm disinheriting myself. Same result."

"Why didn't you just tell me that?"

He shrugged. "I wanted to see if you'd stick around. And I didn't want to wonder if your reason for staying was to try to convince me to keep it."

She sighed, lowered her head, then brought it up again as if something new had occurred to her. "So then you...want me to? Stick around?"

"Is that not obvious?"

"No. I figured you were just spying on me for Rob." She shrugged a shoulder. "And I wouldn't blame you if you were. Payback's a bitch."

"I *am* spying on you for Rob. He wants to know why you really came home and whether your father knows about the baby."

"I came for family," she said softly. "And that's the absolute truth. And no, Jack doesn't know about the baby, but I'm going to tell him the next time I have the chance to talk to him."

"Have the chance to talk to him? That's a funny way to put it. Where is Jack, these days?"

She shook her head. "He doesn't generally give me his itinerary, Dax. I don't know where he is."

"Well, now I know why you're here and what your father knows. Mission accomplished. I am no longer spying on you for Rob." Now he was only spying for himself, he thought with a pang of guilt. Impulsively, he moved closer to her, reached out very slowly, and brushed a wisp of hair off her face, tucking it behind her ear. It was a knee-jerk apology. He felt bad leading her on, even though he was pretty sure she was doing the same to him.

And he was a little bit afraid he was only pretending to be leading her on, trying to fool himself into believing that. And failing.

She met his eyes, blinked. "You're way too easy on me."

"I can't seem to help myself." He leaned closer. Leaned wasn't the right word. He was pulled, like she was wearing magnets under her skin and he was made of metal. She tipped her chin up just the tiniest bit, just enough to tell him yes, so he kissed her. He wrapped his arms around her waist and pulled her tight to him, and he kissed her.

Everything he'd ever felt for her came flooding back in a rush that suffused him from his head to his toes with warm, red glitter, dusted in cinnamon. It had been there all along. He'd just bagged it up and hoisted it into the attic, out of sight. But then, *bam*! One kiss. Glitter avalanche.

It scared him, but his fear was hopelessly buried.

Her lips were soft, and her mouth was wet and she tasted like jalapenos. He kissed her deeper. Her hands were on his shoulders, but they didn't twine around his neck the way they used to. She kept moving them down over his arms, then back up and over to his chest, as if she couldn't make up her mind whether to push him away or pull him closer.

Eventually, he lifted his head. "I'm going to refuse the inheritance. I want you to know that."

"I know," she said, a little bit breathlessly, and then, "But doesn't that mean it'll go to the SRA?"

Like a bucket of ice water, those words. He stepped back a little, blinking at her. "Since when do you know so much about Aurora Springs horseracing, Kendra?"

Her eyes flared, just the tiniest bit. Just enough to make his stomach knot up. She walked away from him, picking up the empty shopping bags all over the floor.

"Since I started dating the only son of a track owner almost two years ago." She shrugged and looked him square in the eye. "I was a grifter, Dax. That's what we do."

"*Were?*"

She swung away from him angrily, paced hard to the window and leaned on the sill. "I haven't gamed anyone since... since you."

That was a bombshell. If it was true.

But it couldn't be true.

"So then what do you do? You've obviously got money. That Vette—"

"Same thing I always did, just legally now. I do online promotion for little one-and-two woman operations. There are lots of online entrepreneurs these days."

He was gaping. He shouldn't be gaping.

"It started as a favor for a friend whose indie marketing biz grew faster than she could keep up with, and after six months I was really good at it, and started my own little operation. It just...grew into...something." She stopped talking, searched his face. "You don't believe me, do you Dax?"

"I...no. I don't. Sorry."

"Yeah. I don't blame you. God, I need a cigarette." She lowered her butt onto the windowsill. "So you're seriously just gonna give away something worth millions?" she asked.

"My mother owns forty-nine percent of the track, you know."

Her eyebrows rose, and she did too, right off the windowsill. She stood there blinking at him like she was a kid and he'd just told her Santa wasn't real.

"No. I didn't know that."

She lowered her head. Her hair fell like a pale silk curtain around her face. Then she ran her hand over her forehead, pushing all that hair up and catching it behind her head. "I've always liked Caroline." She looked him in the eye, then looked away, shaking her head and letting go of her hair. It fell around her shoulders, over her arms.

"She liked you, too."

Kendra nodded, then seemed to shake herself. "Let's go find something to eat. I'm starved." She walked past him into the hall and down the stairs.

He'd thought if he was honest with her, she might be inclined to reciprocate. But she was still keeping things from him. And from that reaction, they were big things. The look on her face when he'd mentioned his mother—hell, this was looking bad. This was looking worse by the minute.

~

It could've been awkward, staying for dinner and a movie with Kiley and Rob and Dax. Kendra had expected it to be awkward. But it wasn't. It was almost nostalgic, being back in the house again. Even with all the updates and fresh paint and furniture, it was still the place where she and Kiley had spent their childhood. She felt at home there. They ate in front of the TV and watched a DVD of *Planes, Trains and Automobiles*. The film had cracked them up when they'd watched it every Thanksgiving as kids, and still did.

Afterwards, the guys cleaned up, leaving her and Kiley alone in the big living room. They were more or less out of earshot, due to running water, rattling dishes and deep male voices. That was when Kiley finally said, "So how's Dad?"

Kendra should've been ready for the question, but she wasn't. It rocked, because she didn't know how Jack was. She didn't even know for sure he was still alive. "Oh, you know Jack," she said at length. It was an answer without being a lie.

"Yeah, I do. He's always okay, isn't he?"

"Somehow or other, he always is."

Kiley was quiet for a long moment. Then, "Does he hate me?"

"Come, on, Kiley. Jack doesn't hate. He's an easy-going charmer." She shrugged. "He *was* good and pissed once he realized how you'd played him. Broke the cardinal rule of scam."

"Never play family." Kiley quoted it in her father's exact inflections. "I know."

"He got over it, though. By the time we'd made it back to Jersey, he was saying you were just like Mom. And he loved her, so...."

Kiley nodded. "He always said I was more like Mom, and you were more like him."

"It always made me crazy jealous, too," Kendra admitted.

"I was jealous of *you*. You always made him so proud, and I just always messed up."

"Why can't parents just let their kids be who they are without feeling the need to comment and critique?" Kendra asked.

"I'm gonna do that with Diana."

"That's good, cause I'm gonna get her some things from the boy side of the sexist toy store. That nursery needs a little...balance."

Kiley blinked at her, then got the not so subtle message and nodded. "You're right. It's pretty princessed-up in there, isn't it?"

"A little bit," Kendra said. "So what about you?"

"What *about* me?"

"You and Jack. Do you hate him?"

Kiley widened her eyes. "Of course I don't hate him, he's my father." She hugged her belly with both arms as she said it.

"If you don't hate him, how can you not tell him he's having a granddaughter?"

Kiley pressed her lips tight. "I love my father, Kendra. But I love my baby more. Look at the life she's going to have. Look at this place, at what Rob and I have waiting for her. A warm, safe home. A thriving business. A great big extended family. A hometown where she'll never have to feel too ashamed to hold her head up. And two parents who adore her and each other." She shook her head slowly and said, "Dad could mess it all up."

"And so could I. That's what you think, isn't it?"

"No."

"Then why didn't you tell me?"

Kiley lowered her head. "I was still deciding when and how to tell you. But I was going to. Rob knows I was, so does Dax. You can ask them. You know neither of them would lie."

"I don't know anything of the kind. Rob asked Dax to find out what I was up to. Did you know that?"

She sat straighter in her chair. "No, I didn't."

"Well, he did."

Kiley frowned toward the kitchen, then at her sister again. "He was trying to protect me and the baby."

"Protect you? From me? Kiley, I'm your sister, Diana's aunt."

"We had a nice evening, Kendra. Why can't you just let it be?"

Kendra pressed her lips and tried to push down her hurt. She hadn't realized just how deep it ran. Here she was lecturing her sister, who was only days away from giving birth, if that. It wasn't the time.

She took a deep breath, held it a second, then blew it out entirely. "You're right. I'm sorry."

"I'm the one who should be apologizing to you," Kiley said. "I love you, and I've missed you. I didn't know how much until you showed up again. I want you to stay for Thanksgiving."

"Only if we order takeout. You're in no condition to make a feast, sis, and you know I don't cook."

"I'm not making it. It's a family thing. The Brand half of the family used to do it out at Bobby Joe and Vidalia's farmhouse, but the clan has outgrown it. This year they're closing down The Long Branch for the day and we're all gathering there."

Kendra lowered her head. "I'd fit into that like a hooker in church."

"I want you there. It feels odd not having anyone from my past, my family. I'm tired of it."

She knew she wasn't going to stay for Thanksgiving, but figured she had upset her pregnant sister enough for one night. "We'll see. That's as much of a commitment as you're gonna get out of me right now."

"Okay."

"It's getting late," she said. "I'm gonna head back, let you get some sleep."

Kiley started to get up, but Kendra beat her to it, hopped to her feet and leaned over her, kissed her cheek. "Night, Kiley." Then she laid a hand on her bulging belly. "Night, Diana."

Something thumped against her palm, and a bubble of delight expanded in her chest. "I think she just high-fived me," she said. "Clearly she agrees about that girlie nursery." She softened the words with a wink, and then headed out through the kitchen to say goodbye to Rob.

Dax said, "I'll walk you out."

∽

They sauntered along, side by side, to her little Corvette. His Charger was parked beside it. He'd enjoyed the evening with Rob and Kiley, and his heart yearned to have what his best friend had. A wife. A home. A family.

"So?" he asked. "Things okay with you and Kiley?"

She shrugged. "I think so, yeah."

"You ever gonna tell me the story behind your sweet ride?"

"You won't believe me."

"Try me," he said.

She sighed. "It's the first thing I bought with my honestly earned-money."

He frowned at her, because she was completely sincere. Not a sign of the mask other people couldn't see through. And she sounded proud.

"Told you you wouldn't believe me."

"I...I kind of do."

"It's true. You play your cards right, I might even let you drive it."

"We can take it up on the back roads. There's a spot up there makes a nice dirt track, if you ever want to burn off some steam."

"Yeah? You do that? Race around a dirt track to burn off steam?"

"Better than drinking," he said.

She smiled and it felt easy between them, somehow. "You heading home, too?" she asked, and then before he could answer, "Where is home, anyway? I just realized, I don't even know where you live."

"I'm renting a trailer about a mile that-a-way," he said, nodding in the general direction. "Nothing fancy. I've been kind of drifting here. Not sure where I was going or what I wanted to do with my life."

"And now?" she asked.

"Now, I know exactly what I want." He looked at her and smiled. "A goodnight kiss. You amenable?" He turned toward her, leaned down, expecting her to lean up.

Instead, she opened the car door and slid inside, started it, and drove away. Her window lowered and she gave a sassy finger wave back at him.

He stood there until her taillights vanished in the distance.

When Kendra pulled into The Long Branch, the parking lot was packed. Yellow light and country music spilled out of the place like honey dripping from a beehive. She drove around back, where the owners and tenants parked. But she didn't go up the outside stairs to her room. Instead, she walked around to the front, moseyed on through the batwing doors, paused and took a look around. Last night she'd listened to the success of this place. Tonight, she was going to see it firsthand.

Cowboys, locals, she'd bet, in their finest authentic western wear, out to score a few tourist honeys, and there were tourist honeys by the carload.

She crossed to the bar. A smiling blonde she didn't know was behind it, and brought her a whiskey almost as quick as she'd asked for one. Kendra slammed it, and tapped her finger on the glass.

The waitress brought her another. "You okay?" she asked as she set the shot glass down.

"Yeah, I'm good."

Her phone buzzed. She downed the second shot, and the bar chick held up the bottle and her eyebrows. Kendra held up a forefinger for "just one more" and pulled her phone out of her jeans. She knew that number, glowing on the screen. It was the same number the bastard holding her father had called from before. Seeing it made her stomach clench. She tapped the green button, brought the phone to her ear. "Give me a minute to get private."

She picked up the refilled glass, and said, "Can I take this one to my room?"

"Sure can," the waitress replied.

So Kendra took the third whiskey toward the dining room and up those elegant, carpeted stairs that fanned out at the bottom. It was a damn pretty place.

Once back in her room, she figured less than the requested

minute had passed. She sat on the bed, put the glass on the nightstand, and heeled off her shoes. It had been a long freaking day. She was exhausted.

Twisting her mouth in distaste, she picked up her phone again. "Okay, I can talk now."

"It's about time. I want a status report."

Vester Caine's voice was high pitched, for a man. It always sounded vaguely whiny to her, which was funny, because Vester Caine didn't whine. He was the biggest bully in the schoolyard. He made other people whine.

"I want to talk to Jack."

"I want a report. Now. Have you convinced him to accept his inheritance?"

She sighed, but didn't want to do anything to set the bastard off. "The lawyers are coming out here to deal with the will."

"When?"

"I don't know. It's almost Thanksgiving, you know, people take time off—"

"Then help 'em to see the urgency of the situation."

"I'm trying." She was angry. This guy was going to die slow when she got her hands on him. She'd never thought she had it in her to hurt someone physically, but she was pretty sure she could make an exception for this pig.

"The track bookkeeper says Russell's got an outside accountant snooping around the books. Get him to call it off."

"The track's regular bookkeeper works for you?" So it was something to do with finances behind Caine's interest in Aurora Downs.

"Get him to call the guy off," he repeated.

"How the hell am I supposed to do that?"

"Figure it out. Or maybe your old man sleeps naked in the meat locker tonight."

"I'll figure it out."

"Good girl. Just get Dax Russell to accept that inheritance, relax and let business go on as it always has. You get him to stand down, Kendra, or your old man dies. You got me? I'll kill him." He ended the call.

Kendra put her phone on the nightstand and picked up the whiskey.

CHAPTER FIVE

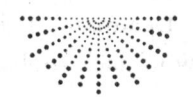

Jack Kellogg had a full house, and a face that was his best weapon. It was handsome, the face of a lovable rogue, when he wanted it to be. That was the one women usually fell for, and when necessary, he could morph into heartbroken hero or rugged protector. But lovable was his favorite. It made for a fun boyfriend stage and usually a bigger payoff in the end.

His poker face was legendary. He didn't sit stoic as a rock, wearing a blank stare. He didn't change a thing. Just kept on being Jack Kellogg, rapier-witted ladies' man, a living legend among both flim and flam, currently a guest in an ordinary farmhouse in Middle-of-Nowhere, Oklahoma.

Vester Caine kept the place for when he needed an off-the-grid spot to conduct the messier parts of his business. Which was fairly often, Jack figured. Caine was one of the top heroin importers in the northeast. But you don't defecate where you eat, as the saying goes. And this place was close to the current action.

Jack pushed a few more poker chips to the center of the table, leaned back in his seat, and wished he hadn't given up cigars. The other guys were puffing away on some Cubans that smelled like heaven.

"Maybe I'll have to talk to my daughter myself," he said. "You're just pissing her off."

"You'd give it away." Vester sucked the cigar slow and deep, rolled the smoke around on his tongue without letting any escape. "She knows you too well."

"*Me. I'd* give it away." Deadpan. "This was my idea. I'm not gonna be the one to blow it." Jack took a cigar from the nearby humidor—it was okay because Caine had offered one earlier—and ran it under his nose, sniffing it up like good cocaine. Not that he did that anymore, either.

Getting older sucked. And you couldn't con Father Time, no matter how good you were.

"Kendra starts to doubt my well-being, you don't know what she might do," he added for good measure.

"I could bench press her with one hand. What's she gonna do?" Caine set his cigar on the edge of an ashtray, still studying his cards.

"Bench pressing my kid isn't part of our deal." If he thought Vester Caine might actually kill him, as he'd threatened to do on the phone with Kendra, he wouldn't have been quite so relaxed. That wasn't going to happen, though. He had approached Caine with a plan to get the man something he needed, and would pay very well for. Caine had been laundering heroin money through Aurora Downs for fifteen years. If Dax Russell didn't inherit his father's track, it would go to the State Racing Association, they'd go through the books and find tens of millions of dollars worth of discrepencies. So Caine needed Dax to inherit. And Jack knew his daughter could get Dax to do anything she wanted him to do. The guy was nuts about her.

So he brought his idea to Caine within hours of hearing about the elder Russell's death. He and Caine were both businessmen. This was a civilized, mutually beneficial arrangement. It should go off without a hitch.

On the other hand, Vester Caine was a killer, and patience was not his strong suit.

Jack tucked the cigar into his breast pocket. *I'll just keep you nearby, Stogie, in case this thing goes south.*

Ace laid his cards down. "I'm ou-ou-out." Then he sneezed. Again.

Ace looked like you'd expect a guy with a nickname like Ace to look. He embraced the whole gangster-greaser cliché without apology. Slicked hair, leather jacket, inked forearms. But his chronic allergies blew the image to hell. He ran into the bathroom for another Benadryl. The guy started sneezing and snotting every eight hours like clockwork, then popped an allergy capsule and got over it.

"I call." The dough-faced ginger named Phil was Vester's right-hand man. You didn't see too many dough-faced gingers named Phil in the heroin business, but that was probably a benefit. Phil pushed in a stack of chips. He looked like the kind of guy who'd fold every hand. But Jack had seen him stab a man to death with a rusty metal file because he didn't have a knife handy. He was brutal.

And he was smart, too. Dangerous combination.

Jack dropped two cards into his lap, produced two more from his sleeve, and programmed his handsome features to reflect abject disappointment. "You saw right through my bluff, didn't you Phil?"

"Every fucking time." Grinning, Phil hauled all his chips in. "You better be good for this, Kellogg."

"I'm good for it, and you know it."

"How do I know it?"

"Because your boss is gonna be paying me handsomely once Kendra's boy-toy inherits his old man's racetrack."

"That's right," Vester said. "And if she fails, you don't need to worry about collecting, Phil. We'll take it out of his hide."

"Hey, hey, now, that's not part of the deal either," Jack said.

Vester sent him a wink. "Relax. You said your girl could charm this Russell fellow out of his liver if she put her mind to it. You telling me that wasn't true?"

"I'm not stupid enough to lie to you, Caine."

"Then you got nothing to worry about. And it's Mister Caine. Show some respect."

～

"Change of plans," the text message said. "Meet at OK Corral." It came from a number Kendra didn't recognize, and had a cc line of a thousand.

Okay, four.

"Same time?" someone texted back.

Thumbs-up sign. "C U there."

She knew Sophie and Emily would be there, and assumed one of them was the initial sender. Maybe Allie Wakeland, the pregnant friend, was the third. But she wondered who the fourth number on the cc line belonged to. She supposed she'd find out when she got there.

She turned the 'Vette onto Main Street and slowed to a crawl as she watched the town she'd grown up in take shape around her. First she passed the giant circle of park. The road split around it, one lane circling it on the right, the other on the left, and then met again on the other side. Nothing much had changed on Main Street. The Big Falls Diner looked just like it had when they'd moved east. Rosie was running the place like she always had, and never seemed to age. Everyone called her Aunt Rosie. It was a Big Falls thing. The bank hadn't changed its window décor since the 1890s, by the look of it. The drug store was still where it belonged. Someone had put in a comic book store—she'd have to check that out. And that photo studio was new must be Allie Wakeland's. It used to be a hardware store, she thought. Edie Brand was the only other photographer in town, but her studio was in her home out by the Falls. The bakery was still the only business that sported a pink and white striped awning instead of green and white like everyone else. It had always been a bakery with the wrong color awning. It had been Myrtle's before it was Sunny's, back when Kendra and Kiley were kids. Someone had put up a coffee shop on the corner, the kind that served fancy brews, but not a chain. They didn't allow chains in Big Falls. But she could see how that might change now that the place had a couple of bona fide tourist attractions. She hoped not, though. Big Falls wasn't a chain kind of a town. It was more of a Norman-Rockwell-goes-west kind of a town. More an honest-upright-people-live-here kind of a town.

More a too-good-for-the-likes-of-Kendra-Kellogg kind of a town.

She wasn't comfortable here. Never had been.

She pulled off Main street and into the parking lot that the OK Corral shared with the next business, Armstrong's Garage. She tried to remember the name of the guy who'd owned it when she was a kid and came up blank. Not Armstrong. It had been a long time.

A black van with a batman logo on the side pulled in beside her. She frowned at the design for about ten seconds before she got it. It was a V, not a bat. Vet Mobile. Cute. Then Doc Sophie pulled in and then a pickup truck. The woman who got out was older—how much older, it wasn't possible to say. Her hair was long, curly, and black with silver strands. She was short and curvy, and not someone Kendra would ever think about conning. You learned early on in the confidence game how to read people. If you didn't, you were doomed. Kendra would not bet against this one, not on her life.

Another car pulled in, and Allie Wakeland got out, belly leading the way. They all hugged, Sophie and Emily and Allie, and the lady. And then they all turned her way, arm in arm, smiling.

Kendra said, "Um, good morning?"

"Morning!" they broke like a football huddle, the ruler coming forward with her hand out. "Vidalia Brand," she said. Oh, that made sense. The matriarch. "I'm glad you're here for the birth of your niece. Sisters need each other at a time like this."

Allie had come up to stand beside her, and Kendra thought it was a deliberate move, like she was saying, "Don't worry, I'll be your ally."

And then another woman, a sunshine blonde, came trotting along the sidewalk with a big pink and white striped cardboard box.

"That's Sunny Cantrell," Allie said when the walking ray of sunshine got close enough.

"From the bakery, right?" Kendra asked.

Sunny nodded. "Nice to meet you, Kendra."

"Sunny's doing baby shower cupcakes," Vidalia Brand said. Then, "There's food in the truck girls."

Kendra got swept into the tide of grown women scurrying to obey the alpha, while Vidalia unlocked the saloon to let them all in. Soon she was carrying a covered Tupperware platter and heading into the dim interior of the OK Corral. It was a much more downscale bar than The Long Branch, obviously meant for the locals, not the tourists. Rich wood tones were everywhere, from the bar to the racks behind it, to the woodwork to the flooring. There were tables and booths, a kitchen in the back for bar food, and wagon wheel light fixtures lining the ceiling.

Vidalia removed the chairs from on top of a big round table and gave it a wipe down. Then they unloaded the food and

Kendra sniffed the air. "Am I dreaming or do I already smell coffee?"

"I set the auto-timer," Vidalia said. "Should be fresh and ready." The others had scattered, returning quickly with plates, silverware, cream and sugar, and blessedly large coffee mugs. And then they sat around that table and dug in. Vidalia moved around them, pouring their mugs full before sitting down herself.

Kendra sat there a second. "I did not expect a full-blown breakfast."

"This family's big on food," Doc Sophie said. "They're all gonna be on cholesterol meds by sixty."

"Fortunately, I don't believe in age," Vidalia said. "Or prescriptions." She speared a sausage link with her fork. All the food was piping hot and abundant, including the gooey cinnamon buns Sunny had brought from the bakery.

The chit-chat was friendly, but minimal for a while, because they were all too busy eating to talk.

"So," Emily began when the eating had begun to wind down. "I made you a copy of everything we've agreed on so far." She handed a folder across the table. It had printed pages with holes punched. Wow. Efficient. "That doesn't mean any of it is carved in stone. You're running the show now, Kendra."

Vidalia got up and started clearing plates, and when Emily rose to help, she held out a hand. "No, no, you plan. This won't take a minute." She was as good as her promise, whisking away everything but the coffee mugs and returning with a fresh pot to refill them.

"Yeah, well…to be honest I've never done anything like this before, so I'm sure whatever you've got started is fine." Kendra was running her fingertip down a bulleted list:

- Date: November 20th
- Time: 3 PM

- Place: The Long Branch dining room
- Catering: Chef Ned
- Cake: Sunny (cupcakes)
- Menu: To be determined.
- Invitiations:

Her finger stopped there. "It doesn't say anything next to invitations."

"Oh, the invitations! They arrived yesterday. I tucked 'em away." Vidalia hustled behind the bar and came out with a box, set it in front of Kendra and took off the lid. "They need to go out today, if possible. But we don't have a complete guest list yet."

Kendra unfolded blotter paper to see a stack of invitations laid out flat. The front showed a cartoon baby princess riding a unicorn with sparkles and glitter all around her. Of course it did. God, she loved her sister, but pregnancy sure gave her girlie side a shot of rocket fuel, and apparently her friends all knew it.

They'd probably seen the nursery.

"We've been trying to figure a way to get a list from Kiley's side of the family without giving away the surprise," Emily said.

Kendra's head came up. "Kiley's side?"

"Your side," Sophie clarified. "Now that you're here, you can fill in the blanks. It's co-ed, so Rob and the guys can attend, too."

Kendra thought of Uncle Willie and Fat Carl and Miss Dolly. And she thought of Jack, too. He should be at this thing. It was for his first grandchild, a baby girl named after the only woman he'd ever loved, their mom.

And yet Kiley didn't want him to know, and it wasn't fair, and the fact that he could end up dead almost any time now made it feel even worse.

She wouldn't let him die without knowing, she decided it for sure right then. Maybe she could get him out of there in time.

Maybe she could convince Kiley to let him come to the shower. But at the very least, she was going to let him know.

Dammit, Kiley needed to remember who the hell she was. She was not one of these too-good-to-be-true country gals, pretty and smart and honest and kind. They probably had perfect houses and perfect husbands and perfect lives and perfect kids.

She pictured her sister in that pretty little farmhouse, the flowerboxes, the business she'd started, the happy kitchen, the amazing husband.

Yeah, maybe she was. Maybe she was. That part of her had come from their mother, who Kiley had idealized in her mind.

But she was also the daughter of Jack Kellogg. She was the notorious Kendra Kellogg's twin. She'd been raised by hucksters and scammers and petty criminals. She needed to respect that part of her heritage.

Kendra couldn't invite anyone from their childhood, though. Not if it would ruin the shower for Kiley.

Then she remembered the soft smile in her sister's eyes when she'd mentioned Miss Dolly, and how she'd said she missed having her family around. It might be okay. "I do have one name we can add to the list," Kendra said.

"Oh good!" Sunny handed her a pen. "Jot down the name and address."

"Kiley's gonna be so surprised," Allie said.

"Yeah," Kendra said. "Surprised." And she knew it would either make her sister's day or ruin it. She bit her lip, but in the end, thought the potential payoff was worth the risk. She would make it her personal task to ensure Miss Dolly behaved herself.

~

Dax had invited Kendra to come out to lunch with him, and she had agreed eagerly. She had a lot of talking to do and not much time to do it in, and she'd figured out how to use the planning to ask questions.

They sat in the clearing next to the waterfall, with a picnic spread out on the ground—red-and-white checked blanket, wicker basket and all. She was sure Dax had help putting it all together. Probably from her sister. Cold fried chicken, extra sharp cheese, root beer in glass bottles. Root beer always tasted better from glass bottles.

"You said your mom and the lawyers are coming out," she said. "When are they arriving?"

"Why?" he was instantly suspicious.

She'd hoped he might be starting to trust her a little bit. No such luck. It made her angry that he assumed she was up to something, but that didn't make much sense, since she was, in fact, up to something.

"I want to invite her to Kiley's shower." She tipped her head. "I could hardly come up with anyone from our side of the family. Not that she is, really, but you work with Rob, so I figured…."

"Oh." He blinked, and then his features relaxed again. "I think she'd love to be invited. When's the shower?"

She made a face. "This weekend. Short notice, right?"

"Mom's arriving tomorrow. I bet she'd be grateful for an excuse to stay a while." He gave her a gentle smile. "She's gonna be so happy to see you again."

She'd tried hard to avoid meeting Dax's mother when they'd been fake-dating the first time around. But eventually she had. Caroline was as petite and luminescent as a Christmas elf. She smiled with her whole being, and her big brown eyes contrasted with her platinum-or-maybe-silver short short hair in a way that could make curmudgeons want to hug.

"Even though I screwed her only son over and came between him and his old man?"

"What came between me and my old man was my old man."

He put a hand over one of hers. "She was pretty pissed when she found out about your kidney scam, Kendra, I gotta be honest about that. But we've talked about it a lot since then, and she's over it."

Kendra frowned at him, trying to read his face, which was usually easy to do. He averted his eyes this time. "Why is she over it? What did you tell her about me?"

"You want that last piece of chicken?" He reached for it as he asked the question.

She snatched it before he could, and shook it at him. "You didn't give her my motherless-child, daddy-in-prison, ward-of-the-state sob story, did you?"

"I want to hear more about your boyfriend turned stalker," he said. "You said he was the reason you let everyone believe you'd died in that fire."

She took a big bite of the chicken, chewed it slow, then chugged some of the root beer to give herself time to think. "It wasn't a big deal. I hate talking about it."

She handed him the rest of the chicken leg. He took it from her, but set it down instead of eating it, and leaned back on his elbows, watching her, waiting for her to fill in the details.

She heaved a giant sigh. "He was a mark I never should've messed with. Had whatever gene it is some men have that makes them control freaks when it comes to women. When he realized he'd been had, he started parking outside my place to watch me. Followed me around, stole my cell phone, a bunch of shit like that."

Dax sat up slow, riveted, his face searching hers.

"He dragged me into his car one day. Had a gun. Told me it was over. That he was going to end us both. I put on my seat belt, jerked the wheel and stomped on his gas-pedal foot. We hit a tree. Then while he was seeing little birdies from the impact, I got out and ran for it. The fire at the halfway house happened that night. They identified another girl who'd been there visiting as me. I figured it was best to stay dead, given the asshole was still alive and still bat shit crazy."

He was upright now, food forgotten. He looked like he wanted to hug her, the big angel.

"And what about now?"

"I don't know. It's no secret I'm alive. It made the news, the mistaken identity angle, you know? But I haven't seen or heard from him again."

"That's...a lot to have hanging over your head."

"I've put it behind me. Frankly I think news of my death probably smacked him upside the head a little bit. He was questioned about the fire by the cops, while the cause was still undetermined. Turned out it was accidental, but that might've given him enough of a scare to make him leave me alone." It was enough with the heavy stuff, she thought. "So, it's your turn to answer my question. You told your mom my sob story, didn't you?"

He nodded slow. "I did."

"Hell. I hate pity."

"You'd rather she go on hating your guts for breaking her only son's heart? Trust me, this is way better."

"Baaaaah." She started picking up the dishes. Dax snatched the remainder of the chicken leg before she grabbed his plate. She put everything in a plastic bag and tucked the bag into the picnic basket. "So now what?"

"Now, we enjoy a few minutes of bliss before my mother and the lawyers descend and the baby shower planning resumes."

"Bliss, huh?"

"Yep. Big Falls bliss. It's the best kind." He took the picnic basket to his car and put it in the back seat, then returned to the blanket while she sat there, watching him. He stretched out on his back, hands behind his head. "Perfect. Come here. Stretch out beside me, right here." He patted the blanket beside him before returning his hand to its spot, where it served as his pillow.

She scooted closer and stretched out, but she kept her knees bent up, and only lowered herself as far as her elbows.

"Aw, come on now. Lie back or it's all wrong. What are you, afraid I'll pounce on you?"

"Of course not."

"Afraid I won't?" He asked it with a wiggle of his brows that made her laugh and give in. She lay down, putting her hands behind her head, and straightened her legs out, crossing them at the ankles.

The new position put the thundering waterfall directly into her line of sight.

"You've barely noticed the falls since we've been here," he said. "All you've been seeing is the whirlwind going on inside your head."

"I noticed the falls." It would've been impossible not to hear their roar. But he was right, it had only been background noise. She hadn't really looked at the waterfall. She looked now. The water wasn't just one color, but a hundred. Dark slate gray here, crystalline there, frothy and white somewhere else. And the way the sun hit the cascade created a rainbow in the air in front of them. Had she really been having lunch under a rainbow for the past hour and not even seen it?

She took a deep breath and let her muscles unclench a little bit. Her head relaxed back onto her hands, and she gazed at the rainbow and thought of how her sister had always believed in angels and fairies, the Easter Bunny and Santa Claus, and how she used to tease Kiley over it. Kendra had never believed a word of it. She'd seen it all as a con that parents played on their kids. In her mind, her father's voice repeated one of the gems of parental wisdom he'd shared over and over with his daughters.

There are two kinds of people in this world, girls. Players and marks. People who don't know that are always marks. People who do know it, well, they get to choose. Do you want to be the girl crying in her pillow 'cause she got taken, or the one walkin' away with a wad of cash, whistlin' Dixie?

There was a third kind of person though. The kind who walked away with a wad of cash *and* sobbed into her pillow. Kiley had been one of those. But only for a little while. Eventually she'd chosen to be neither a mark nor a con. She'd chosen to be a good person who knew the score. She was street tough and savvy. And she knew how to run a game. She was also a happy wife, a business owner, a local hero and about to be a mamma.

How the hell did she *do* that?

"Hey."

"What?"

"You're in your head again," Dax said. "If that waterfall can't keep your attention, there must be something more than baby shower planning on your mind."

"Yeah." She looked at him. His blue eyes were deep and full of tender strength. She'd always loved that about him, that sense of power, and of his kind soul holding its reins with easy confidence. There was something comforting about that.

"You want to tell me about it?"

She pursed her lips. Time to launch. She needed him to keep the track, and stop poking around in the books. *Deep breath, look him in the eyes and lie like you mean it.*

"I've got this idea. I mean, it's …like the greatest idea ever. But I'm afraid if I tell you, you'll think I'm trying to play you again."

He rolled onto his side toward her, studied her face like if he looked deep enough into her eyes, he could see her thoughts. "But you're gonna tell me anyway."

"I think I have to. I told myself I was gonna be honest with you this time, Dax. If I didn't tell you, that wouldn't be honest." She sighed and lowered her eyes, then met his again, and gave a deliberately tremulous smile.

He seemed mesmerized by her lips all the sudden. She tipped her chin a millimeter, to tell him yes, and he kissed her just like she knew he would. He kissed like a man who loved kissing. She loved the way his thick lips moved sensually over hers, parting and closing in ultra-slow motion.

Her brain melted, every thought just drained away. This was what could shut off the maelstrom of thoughts always swirling inside her mind. This. Nothing else, not a horseback ride or a waterfall rainbow or her sister's cold fried chicken, could smother her brain into silence the way Dax's kiss could.

She kissed him back, and they started fumbling with each other's clothes the way they'd always done. Such sweet familiarity, the way she unbuttoned his shirt and ran her hands and lips over his chest, until he gently pulled her up and returned all of it back to her. They shucked their jeans, and underthings and wrapped their arms and legs around each other, kissing and rubbing, and rolling every now and then, so he was on top and then she was and then he was again. And when neither of them could stand to wait anymore, they made love; sweet, slow, tender, passionate love. And it was even better than before.

After the second time she whispered his name against his neck and held him while he lost his mind, she wondered if it really was that. *Love*making. And she wondered why fate was so mean, to force her to have to play him again when he was the only man who'd ever made her feel this way.

They lay there, all wrapped up in each other, and it was the middle of the afternoon, and someone could come along at any time. Maybe someone had; she wouldn't have known. She grabbed his shirt off the ground nearby and pulled it over her.

"Gee thanks, just leave me out here for all the world to see," Dax said. But he whispered it as he pushed her hair off her face, and kissed her forehead.

She reached down for one of the shirt's sleeves, and draped it over his junk. "Better?"

"Immensely."

She sighed. Orgasm releases oxytocin in a man's brain, a chemical that makes them want to bond. Now was the best possible time, even though she hadn't planned it that way. "So, can I tell you my idea now?"

He blinked like when someone claps their hands in front of your face. Then he sighed, heavily, closed his eyes and listened.

"I want you to accept your inheritance and let me run the race track for you."

CHAPTER SIX

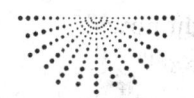

Dax felt as if she'd taken a knife and jammed it right into his heart. She was after the track. He fell onto his back, and all the air rushed out of him. *Damn, damn, damn.*

"Look," she said, pulling his shirt on around her, and springing to her feet. "I keep seeing what Kiley and Rob have done with the ranch. My God, it's fantastic. And they get along. It hasn't come between them in any way." She moved around grabbing all their clothes, tossing his to him and pulling hers on.

He frowned and looked toward her, just as his jeans came flying his way. He sat up and caught them. "It's brought them closer, Rob says."

"Well, sure it has. And look how well it's doing. You know there's a lot in common between flimflam and marketing. I had never thought of it before, but I'm good at selling, Rob. Really good. I think I might be a promotional *genius.*"

He put on his shorts, then his jeans. It was damn chilly out here now that she wasn't snuggled up beside him. She kept on talking, excited now that she'd got started. "I mean, you were willing to just give it away to the SRA," she said.

"Or to my mother," he said.

"But does she really want it?"

He shrugged. "She never got involved with the running of the business. Just let Dad do what he wanted, and he sent her a check every quarter."

She was quiet for a moment. He waited. "If she was full owner, that would have to change though," she said at length. "Wouldn't she rather be traveling around the world with whoever she's dating right now?"

"She's not *dating* anyone!"

She met his eyes again, a smile in hers. "Uh yeah, she is."

"What are you talking about? When's the last time you saw her?"

"I don't need to see her. She's young and she's gorgeous, and she's funny and smart and entirely self-sufficient. If she isn't dating someone, then there are no sane men left on the planet."

"She would've told me."

"Right, 'cause moms *always* tell their sons about their sex lives."

He winced on the word sex. "Jeeze, Kendra!"

She laughed very softly. He was standing there in his jeans and unbuttoned shirt, and she came right over to him. "You're adorable, you know that?"

He closed his eyes, shook his head, started buttoning up.

"You can pay me a salary. Whatever you think is fair. Split the rest with your mom, or, if it makes you happy, give her all the profits. And believe me, there *will* be profits. She won't have to lift a finger." She bent to pick up the blanket, rolled it into a bundle and tucked it under her arm.

He looked at her, standing there, the waterfall her backdrop, sunshine gleaming on her lemon yellow hair, a rainbow arching right over her head like a sign from above. "You really want to go straight?"

"I'm already there. I mean, I didn't think of it as going

straight, but effectively, I've ben making an honest living for almost a year now. I wasn't lying to you about that."

He shook his head slow. She wanted to go straight like he wanted to rob a bank. She didn't even know what straight was. She was running a game *right now*. How could he believe anything she said?

But he couldn't say no. He still didn't know what the hell she was up to.

"I'll um...I'll have to think about it."

"That's all I can ask," she said. And then she smiled, and he kissed her again.

~

"Kendra? It's me."

"*Jack!*" She was so relieved to hear his voice on the other end of the phone that she almost shouted it. "Did you get away? Where are you? Are you all right?"

"Easy, easy, I'm still here, under armed guard. I'm not getting out of here anytime soon, but I'm safe. We're building a rapport here."

Of course they were. Her father could charm the scales off a snake.

"I'll be all right, as long as you get them what they want."

"Damn straight," another man said from somewhere near her father.

"Good." She paced a few steps, relief temporarily making her neck let her head fall forward. "Can they hear me or just you?"

"Just me, why?"

"What's Dax gonna find in those books, Jack?"

"Did you ever do the *laundry* like I asked?"

So Vester Caine was laundering money through Aurora Downs. If the track went to the SRA, that would be exposed.

Maybe not, though. A fat wad of cash here, a compromising picture there...

She told her inner sharpie to STFU.

"Anyway, I convinced Bruno and The Beast to let me talk to you myself."

"Watch it, Jack," a deep voice rumbled.

First-name basis. Nice work, Dad.

"I told Dax he should accept his inheritance and hire me to run the track for him."

"And he bought that? What, has he got amnesia?"

Where she was concerned, she thought, Dax had something way worse than amnesia. She wasn't going to say that, though. "Not yet he hasn't. I mean, he *knows* me. But credit where it's due, Kiley making good gives him reason to think it's possible for me, too."

He was quiet for a second. Then, "How is she?" And his tone was almost heartbroken, and then he had to ruin it. "The back-stabbing, disloyal little shit."

"She was in love, Dad. Being in love is a form of temporary insanity. You have to let people off the hook for the crap they do while they've got it." It was, word for word, a Jack Kellogg quote. Part of the unwritten code among grifters.

"And you never game your family," he said. "Never."

"Maybe the code needs an edit, since it contradicts itself."

He laughed and it did her heart good to hear it. She took a big breath. Her father could die. She had to tell him. "Kiley's gonna have a baby, Dad."

"Holy fu—mackerel!"

It made her smile. He used to say "Holy fuck" all the time, and as little girls, she and Kiley had called him on it. So they each made up something to say instead. Kiley's was "Holy smokes!" and Kendra's was "Holy guacamole!" because she always had to step it up. Jack, had gone with mackerel.

"When?" he croaked into the phone.

"Before Thanksgiving. It's a girl, and she's gonna call her Diana."

"Jeeze, you want to make me cry in front of these guys, show my belly?"

She smiled. She loved her POS father. So did everyone who knew him. At least for a little while. "This has to go off without a hitch, Kendra. We can't let it touch..." He didn't finish.

"If I'd known, I'd have hooked up with Dax somewhere else. I could've figured a way. Believe me, I'm painfully aware that we brought a flaming pile of manure right to my sister's happy front door." She sighed.

"Jack, time's up," that other voice said. "Come on, the boss'll have us digging our own holes if he finds out we let you talk to her at all."

"Caine's not with you?" Kendra asked.

"Not at the moment. Busy guy."

"Jack, come on!"

"Coming, Ace. I've gotta go," he said. "This time tomorrow?"

"If you can talk 'em into it again," she said.

"Who you think you're talkin' to, girl?"

She smiled. He was right. "This time tomorrow. Listen, I um..." She cleared her throat. "...love you."

She could almost see the dimple in her father's cheek appear, see his smile, and the sparkle in his blue blue eyes that could make women forget their own names. "Me, too."

She disconnected, leaned back in a chair, and released all her breath in a heavy, heavy sigh, as she prepared to sit and contemplate everything he'd said, and everything she had, and try to figure a way out of this mess.

But then there was a heavy knock on her door, and Dax called, "Kendra?" and he sounded off. Just...off.

She got up and opened the door. He stood there, looking like someone had just kicked his puppy, if he had one.

Dax frowned and said, "Mendoza. She says his name is Mendoza."

"Whose name is Mendoza?"

"The guy my mother's been seeing. They're driving in from the airport right now." He paced the room and dropped heavily into the easy chair where she'd been sitting. "I can't believe it. It's been going on for like a year. How could she not tell me?"

Kendra's heart filled with something that felt like warm honey. She moved over in front of him, knelt, and clasped his big hands in hers. "Is she happy?"

He frowned at her. "I don't know."

"Yes, you do. You know your mother better than anyone else on the planet. What did her voice sound like when she told you about this Mendoza?"

She watched him stop the runaway train in his head. She saw him searching his memory, and she saw the moment when he found it, because his gaze softened, and his mouth relaxed into an almost smile. "Yeah," he said. "I think she's pretty happy."

"She'll probably be even happier if you tell her you're okay with it."

"What if I'm not okay with it?"

"Dax, come on. You don't honestly think you get to have an opinion on this, do you?"

He lowered his head. "You're right." Then he finally looked up again. "I'm gonna need you to keep reminding me over and over again, though."

"What's he do, this Mendosa?"

"He's a retired cop." He sighed. "Also, we're having dinner with them."

∼

Look at that handsome sonofabitch.

That's how well Dax's control of his own thoughts was

working when he greeted his mother's boyfriend outside The Long Branch, where they'd gathered for dinner. He'd told himself to look for things to like about Luis Mendoza. He'd told himself his mother was happy and in love and so the guy had to be all right. But his *self* wasn't listening.

He must be ten years younger than she is. What the hell is he after?

"Good to meet you, Dax," he said, extending a hand.

Dax shook, and Luis clasped with both hands, looked him right in the eyes and said, "I've been waitin' a long time to meet you." His accent was smooth Tennessee whiskey. And he had skin the color of burnt gold, and brown eyes surrounded by thick black lashes.

At least he's short.

"Luis wanted me to tell you about us from the start," his mother said. "I just… I don't know. First I was waiting to be sure it would last." She put a hand on Luis's shoulder and they exchanged a lingering look. "It just seemed too good to be true."

When Luis looked at her, his eyes went soft, like their chocolate brown was melting.

"I was sure way before now, of course," she went on. "But by then I was comfortable keeping it to myself and worried about what my only son would think."

"Kendra keeps reminding me, all that matters is what *you* think," he said.

"That would be me," Kendra said. "Nice to meet you, Luis. It's good to see you again, Caroline."

Dax noticed that her tone lacked its usual confidence and her stance had no swagger.

His mother opened her arms, hugged her, and whispered something into her ear. Then she stepped back, clapped her hands and said, "Let's get this show on the road. I'm starving."

"Ned will be happy to hear that," Dax said. "He's the chef, but I don't know that the term wizard isn't more appropriate. What that man can do with a steak'll make you weep."

So they all went inside, two by two. Kendra led the way with Dax's mother right beside her, so he and Luis had to walk together. He knew it was deliberate, he just wasn't sure if it was Kendra's fault or Caroline's. He searched for a topic of conversation.

"This used to be a feed store," he said at last, just as Joe McIntyre came out from behind the bar to greet them. "Bobby Joe McIntyre changed it into this place, ran it with his sons for the first year or so. Now the youngest owns it, lock, stock and barrel. Joe McIntyre, meet my mother Caroline and her .... um ...."

"I never know how to fill that part in either," Luis said easily. "I'm Luis. Good to meet you, Joe. This is a beautiful place." He shook hard while looking around, nodding in appreciation. Then his eyes fell on the player piano and widened. "Is that original Virtuolo?"

"It is!" Joe replied, sounding delighted. "I'll give you a closer look. Let's just get you seated first." He led them through the saloon, past that glorious curved staircase that fanned out at the bottom, through heavy red velvet curtains tied back with gold ropes, and into the dining room. He stood aside as they passed, and once they were in, he undid the tie-backs and the curtains cascaded together. The noise from the barroom was instantly dulled. A few diners were around, but it was early yet.

"McIntyre," Caroline said as Joe held her chair for her. "So then Rob, the one Dax works with, is..."

"My brother," Joey said. "And he's married to Kendra's sister."

"Yes, Kiley, right?"

Everyone nodded, and Joe asked, "How long are you staying in town, Caroline?"

"At least until Kiley's shower. I'm invited." She said it as if bragging, and with a grateful look at Kendra.

Joe frowned. "That's the Sunday before Thanksgiving. You

might as well stay through the holiday. We do it up right around here."

"I bet you do."

He took their drink orders and got them menus, and told them how great the food was, describing several of the dishes right off the top of his head. Dax and Luis got steak. Kendra got a chicken and biscuit meal that looked to die for and his mom ordered quesadillas. And then Joe left them alone and Dax wondered, awkwardly, what the heck they were supposed to talk about.

∽

They sat at a round table, boy-girl, boy-girl, and Kendra automatically tried to read each person present. Force of habit.

Caroline Russell didn't trust her. She wanted to, though. She was friendly and kind, and would give her the benefit of the doubt if Kendra gave her any reason at all. She'd make a great mark with a heart that soft.

It wasn't fair that her dead ex had left her with such a mess. As half-owner of Aurora Downs, she could be implicated in every crime Nealand Russell and Vester Caine had committed. Maybe it was good that Kendra had been dragged into this. Maybe she could find a way to keep the fallout from landing on Dax's mother.

Caroline loved her son way more than she trusted Kendra. So she was watching for slips, and trying to read her expressions and looking deep into her eyes every time they made contact. But she was looking for reasons to believe in her, not the opposite. Caroline wanted to like her. She wanted to like everyone.

Dax hadn't fallen far from the tree. He really was trying to make himself okay with Luis Mendoza, but he *wasn't* okay with him. So he was doing to Luis pretty much what Caroline was doing to her, trying to be nice while on the lookout for lies and ulterior motives. Only Caroline was hoping *not* to find any, while Dax might be leaning the other way.

Mendoza was genuinely besotted with Dax's mother. One of Jack's gems of wisdom, was, "The one thing you can never hide is being in love. The eyes give it away every time." Mendoza's eyes gave it away every time they fell on Caroline.

It made her heart go soft and squishy.

"So Luis, tell us about yourself," Dax said. He tried to sound casual and interested instead of about-to-begin-the-interrogation.

Luis smiled and nodded. "I have a ranch and practice tracks in Tennessee. We train thoroughbreds for their owners." He pulled out a wallet, extracted a biz card, handed it across the table. "Here. So you can Google me later." He grinned. "I want you to, Dax. I'm an open book."

"His place is amazing," Caroline said. "The first time I saw it, I couldn't believe it. It's exactly the kind of place you used to talk about owning someday, Dax." She gazed happily at Kendra. "From thirteen to eighteen, that's all he talked about. Buying a spread, building a practice track and training thoroughbreds."

"He did?" she asked, glancing sideways at Dax.

"I *am* training thoroughbreds. Quarter horses too."

"But not on your own place," his mother said. "Not yet. You will in time. You're meant to. Mothers know these things."

Wow. If that's what he wanted, his dream would be shattered by inheriting his father's racetrack and all its inherent problems —not the least of which was that the biggest heroin importer on the east coast laundered money through it.

"Anything you want to know about me or my business, just ask," Luis went on.

"How old are you?" Dax blurted.

"Dax!" Caroline punched his shoulder. "Shame on you."

"Out of bounds," Kendra muttered, leaning near him and masking it with a cough.

Luis just laughed. "Eleven years younger on paper and a hundred years older in spirit."

Dax seemed to take a moment to digest that. Then he said, "Been married before?"

"Ohforheaven's sakes!" His mother extended her hands and tipped her head up, as if invoking help from above.

Kendra rolled her eyes and pinched the bridge of her nose, looking down.

Luis said, "Seems the ladies are gonna spit roast you no matter how logical your questions, Dax. How 'bout I give you the basics instead of making you ask?"

Dax gave him the palms-up nod to tell him to take it away.

"I was born and raised in Tennessee, always around horses, but nothing big. My father was a jockey. I'm the tallest in my family," he said with a smile at Dax. "So we have that in common. Both big guys."

Luis was 5'9' in boots.

Dax laughed. It was genuine. Kendra saw him try to hold it back and fail.

"I was married for twenty years, to a wonderful woman who died way too young. Breast cancer. Been ten years alone, and then I met your mother at your dad's track on one of my many visits there. It felt like the sun had come out after a decade in the dark. She's my light."

"Holy crap, it must be amazing to be loved like that," Kendra said.

Everyone looked at her and she had a distinct, did-I-say-that-out-loud moment. Then she smirked and added, "If you're into that sort of thing."

Dax glanced her way, his face odd, but then he was back to the third degree. "I'm sorry you lost your wife. Did you have any kids together?"

"No, we tried, but.... Wasn't meant to be, I guess."

And then the food came, and they all stopped talking and dug in. It was too good to allow for much conversation aside from oohs and ahhs and other meal-related exclamations.

It seemed to Kendra that the tension melted away a little bit. Dax relaxed more, his mother did too.

Joe McIntyre came to personally offer them dessert on the house, special dessert menus in hand. Kendra was expecting Dax to say a polite no thanks and end her torture, but instead he said, "Thanks Joe. We'll take you up on that. And we'll have a pot of coffee, too."

"Make mine decaf or I'll never sleep." Caroline was smiling, relieved.

Kendra didn't blame her. If Dax wasn't in a hurry to end the evening, it had to be a good sign as far as his mother was concerned. Kendra was pretty sure it was, unless he'd just thought of a half dozen more questions for the poor guy. But he wasn't like that, her Dax. He was as kind-hearted as they came. Soon he started asking questions that were based on shared interest instead of suspicion, questions about Luis's place, and his training methods, and which owners he'd worked for. Before long, the two of them were trading horse stories. Their frequent rounds of deep, male laughter filled the whole dining room. The other diners around them were smiling, because that sort of thing was contagious. Everybody in the place was just delighted right off their freaking chairs.

Everybody but Kendra.

She was antsy and nervous. There were too many variables at play. If Dax's mother kept reminding him what he really wanted in life, and that it wasn't a racetrack in eastern New York, she was going to have a much harder time convincing him to inherit it.

She'd never known of his dream of owning a training track. It felt like she ought to be nudging him toward that dream instead of trying to get him to turn his back on it. And yet her father could die if she didn't.

Caroline was at considerable risk herself, and that was a new weight on Kendra's shoulders. Dax's mother couldn't possibly know about the money laundering. She wasn't a crook. But that wasn't a legal defense. And she was dating an ex-cop!

She tried to count things that were working in her favor, instead of the opposite, to calm herself down. The lawyers would arrive tomorrow morning, and the meeting was set for tomorrow afternoon. Nothing was likely to happen between now and then that would knock things off course. Dax was leaning toward taking her up on her plan, accepting his inheritance and putting her in as manager. And the first thing she would do was drum up some excuse to fire that outside pencil pusher he had going over the books to placate Caine until she could come up with a more permanent solution.

The very second her father was safe, she was going to tell Dax the truth and find a way to make up for lying to him.

Again.

She couldn't entertain the notion that he might never forgive her for this, because that possibility was too real, and too big, and too inexplicably painful. He had to forgive her. She didn't have a choice here.

Everything would be fine. She just had to get through one more day.

Dax's phone chirped. He pulled it out, read a text message, shook his head, and smiled across at his mother. "Looks like you might be here for Thanksgiving whether you like it or not, Mom." And he looked truly delighted by the notion. "One of the estate lawyers had a family emergency and wants to postpone the meeting until the Monday after the holiday."

Kendra's heart sank into her shoes.

She was doomed.

CHAPTER SEVEN

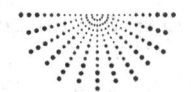

Kendra had not heard from her father again. She'd received only one communication since his phone call—a text message from a blocked number on the day Dax's meeting with the lawyers was supposed to have been.

Is it done?

That was all.

She gnawed her lower lip, thought about lying, decided against it. Who knew if they had someone in their pocket who had ways of verifying? So she told the truth.

Lawyers delayed. Meeting rescheduled.

When?

A week from Monday.

It had been three days since that exchange. There had been no further replies, no phone calls, nothing. She'd been going slowly insane. And there was too much to do today for her to be this distracted. And yet, she was. She needed to talk to her father. And not just to make sure he was still breathing.

Dax's familiar voice followed his soft knock on her door, and everything that was wrought up inside her paused. That had been happening a lot lately. They'd been...hanging out. A lot. They had breakfast together at the diner or at Sunny's Place every morning. And she was usually out at Kiley and Rob's around lunchtime, so they could all eat together. Dinners varied. Sometimes The Long Branch, sometimes the diner. Sometimes at his place, a small, neat trailer where the biggest piece of furniture was the TV. They'd spent a lot of time with Caroline and Luis, and despite him being an ex-cop, Kendra kind of liked the guy.

Aside from that day by the Falls, she and Dax hadn't had sex again. She kept getting all tensed up before it went further than kissing, for reasons she couldn't even identify. And every time, Dax picked up on it and cooled things down. He wouldn't push her. He'd wait for her to tell him when she was ready. That was the kind of guy he was.

She opened the door, and there he was, and in his upturned palm sat a small orange and brown package.

"You brought me a peanut butter cup?"

"You've been stressing out for three days. Thought it might help."

"What you mean to say is, we haven't had sex again for three days."

"You never know. It might help that, too." He lifted the candy bar and wiggled his eyebrows, and there was no way she could stop herself from grinning at him.

She took the treat, tore off the wrapper, and ate one of the two confections, handing him the other. He did not argue. And when they finished their chocolates, he wrapped her up in a great big bear hug and picked her up off her feet.

All the knots in her stomach unknotted. That warm, gooey feeling lubed them up so they just relaxed loose, like they did whenever he was nearby.

"Is anything else wrong? Besides the stress of baby shower planning?"

She lowered her head. "I've been worried about Jack. I haven't heard from him in…a while."

He didn't say anything and she looked up at him. "I know you don't like him, I just…he's my dad, you know."

"I don't *dis*like him," he said. "I don't trust him, that's for sure."

"That's probably for the best," said a little voice from beyond the still open door. And then a wrinkled, smiling woman with a giant flower-decked hat and crooked lipstick peered around Dax's waist. "Hello, honey!"

"Miss Dolly! You came!"

Dax turned sideways, looking down as the small woman crowded past him, her hat barely fitting between him and the doorframe. Kendra had to bend down to hug her. She was a plump lady of maybe four feet ten. Her drawn-on eyebrows were a little too high and she'd colored outside the lines with bright pink lipstick that matched the roses on her wide-brimmed hat.

"Dax, this is Miss Dolly. Miss Dolly, Dax Russell."

"Pleasure to meet you, sir." Dolly swept off her hat, held it to her chest and made a bow. "Wait, that's not right," she said. "*Men* bow. Women…curtsy!" She plunked the big hat back on her head and sketched a wobbly curtsy.

"Pleasure's all mine," Dax said, and returned her curtsy with a bow to play along. He was such a good sport. "Dolly. That's an unusual name."

"Nickname," she said. "My actual name is Clara Bethany."

"Clara Bethany what?"

She waved a small hand. "You couldn't pronounce it." Then she looked him up and down, and wiggled her eyebrows. "Did I *interrupt* anything?"

"No, Miss Dolly," Kendra said. "Stop being naughty. We were just getting ready to head downstairs for some breakfast before I get started decorating for Kiley's shower. You want to join us?"

"But it's already decorated, dear. That hot young bartender with the adorable little girl showed me." Then she frowned and looked way up at Dax. "I didn't imagine that, did I?"

"No," Dax said, "you didn't."

Kendra sent him a look. "What does she mean, the place is all decorated?"

"Me and the boys got up early and decked the place to the rafters. Ned's on top of the food. Sunny's got the cake—"

"Cupcakes," Kendra corrected.

"Rob's gonna see to it that Kiley remains clueless and gets here on time."

"Rob's not supposed to know about this, either."

"He thinks it's a lunch date with the two of us. I told him I needed a wingman."

"Ha!" Miss Dolly said, clapping him on the shoulder. "A big gorgeous hunk like you needs a wingman like I need birth control!" Then she clapped a hand over her mouth and made her eyes big. "Was that inappropriate?"

Kendra just shook her head at Dolly, then returned her gaze to Dax. "You're amazing. I just...thank you. I don't deserve you."

"You seem like you've got a little too much on your shoulders. I thought I could take a little off. Enjoy your reunion with the enchanting Miss Dolly and have fun at your sister's shower. I've got your back. Okay?"

"Yes. *Very* okay."

"I could help with other things too, you know. If you'd let me." He looked into her eyes, and for the first time Kendra got the feeling he knew everything.

But he couldn't. He couldn't know. He was still being kind to her, he couldn't possibly know.

He turned, and tucked Miss Dolly's arm around his on one side, Kendra's on the other, and walked through the hall, and down the staircase. At the bottom, he pulled back the red velvet curtain to reveal the dining room, and said, "Ta-da!"

Pink, purple, and white streamers were draped around the room from a high point in the center, giving it the feel of a castle spire. A mock disco globe spun from the center, throwing shapes within its glimmers, holographic teddy bears and unicorns.

"Emily said *you* picked that out?" Dax said, one brow higher than the other.

"Yeah. I sold out to my sister's penchant for rainbows and unicorns. I'd have preferred gambling and strippers, but it's not my shower."

"It's very nice, dear," Miss Dolly said. "I happen to *like* unicorns."

Dax's mother stood in the center of the room, pointing and making suggestions, while Joe and Jason McIntyre moved a table. She glanced at them and smiled. "How do you like it?" she asked.

"It's beautiful. Thank you for helping."

"Thank you for letting me. I'm having an absolute ball. You know, moos like me, relish opportunities like this."

"Moos?"

"Moms of only sons."

"That's a hoot!" Miss Dolly said, clapping her hands.

"Miss Dolly," Dax said as if remembering her, "this is my mother, Caroline Russell."

"Oh, it's *so* nice to meet you," Caroline all but sang.

"Okay, I'm needed outside. Deliveries to unload." Dax leaned down and kissed his mother on the forehead, and then just as automatically, kissed Kendra on the mouth.

Everyone in the room stopped what they were doing. Oh, they started right up again, but they couldn't hide the fact that they noticed Dax's PDA. He let the curtain fall closed, but Kendra still felt all those eyes on her. Her sister's family-in-law, the brothers McIntyre and Dax's mom.

The saloon end of the place was empty, but way in the back,

a single table was set for two. "I'm gonna let you two ladies enjoy your breakfast," Dax said. "Text if you need me. I won't be far." Then he ducked through the curtain and let it fall behind him.

The kitchen door at the far back of the saloon side, swung opened, and Ned, the chef, stuck his steel gray brush cut out and said, "Ah, perfect timing. Have a seat and prepare yourselves for ecstasy!"

"Ohhh, I like the sounds of *that*." Miss Dolly scurried to her place at the table so fast, Kendra couldn't even keep up. Ned vanished back into the kitchen, the door swinging in and out behind him. Dolly leaned across the table. "The big guy's falling at your feet. Nicely done, Kendra."

"It's not what you think." Then she lowered her eyes. "It is, actually, but I don't have a choice. Vester Caine and a couple of his thugs are holding Jack somewhere."

Her brows would have arched higher, if they could've. "What do they want?"

"It's a long story."

"Don't you worry, we'll fix this." Then she smiled slowly. "We haven't collaborated in forever. It'll be just like old times!"

"Well, right now, I think I have a handle on it, but I'll let you know if I need you." A little of the old thrill tickled at her chest. She said, "Just one thing I need you to remember while you're here, Miss Dolly. This is Kiley's home now."

Dolly pursed up her lips like she'd just sucked a lemon. "Is it true? She's gone straight?"

"Straight as politicians pretend to be." Dolly gave a gentle shudder. "But this is her town, her people, her rules. We can't poach. Not here."

The kitchen door opened, and Miss Dolly looked at Ned as he carried a tray to their table. "Not even a little bit?"

Frowning, Kendra glanced at Ned. He had pronounced cheekbones, where they showed through gray mutton chops that joined up with his mustache. He'd been in the Navy, and looked every bit the salty sea-dog. Turned out he was handsome under all that fluff, if you looked closely enough to see it. Strong jawline. Nice cheekbones. Who knew?

Dolly kicked her softly under the table. "Ow. I mean, oh um, Miss Dolly, this is Ned, the chef here at the Long Branch," Kendra said. "Ned, Miss Dolly, a long-time friend. More than a friend really. She's family."

"Absolutely enchanted," he said, locking eyes with Dolly for an extended moment. She blushed and fanned herself when he turned away to put the tray on a nearby table. Then he unloaded it onto theirs, whisking off domed covers and setting overflowing plates in front of them with a flourish. French toast dripping with melting butter, scrambled eggs, tiny sausages.

"Oh my," Miss Dolly said again.

"I don't get it," Kendra said. "How am I rating all this special treatment?"

"Boss's orders," Ned said.

"Joey?"

"Oh, is that the hottie with the adorable little girl?" Miss Dolly asked.

"Are you trying to make me jealous, Miss Dolly?" Ned asked.

She lowered her head and giggled. "There's no need to be jealous. I prefer my hotties with a little more experience."

"Good to know. Good to know." He was smiling. Kendra didn't think she'd seen crusty old Ned smile in the entire week she'd been staying here.

She cleared her throat to break the flirty smiles they were exchanging, and said, "Dax asked Joe to ask you to do this, didn't he?"

"That is my understanding, yes. He's a good man, Dax is." He turned and got the silver coffee pot off his tray, filled their cups, and set a fresh pitcher of cream on their table. "If there's anything you need..." he began.

"I'll call you," Miss Dolly replied.

"I hope you do, pretty lady." He dipped his head, and then took the tray and returned to the kitchen.

Miss Dolly actually watched his backside as he walked away, and when the kitchen door swung behind him, shook her head and went, "Mm, mm, mm."

"Dolly!"

"What? I'm old, I'm not dead." She fluttered her lashes. She had the kind of perfectly round, baby blue, heavily lashed eyes that always looked vaguely confused. And she used them. Let people think she was a few spots past dotty. Truth was, she was sharp as a tac. She said, "Now tell me what Vester Caine wants." She glanced around. "Digest version. Quietly."

Kendra leaned forward and spoke softly. "Dax's father died and left him a racetrack in Aurora Springs, New York. Law says it has to go to either family or the State Racing Association. Dax doesn't want it. But Caine's been using it to clean money and he wants to keep that going. I'm supposed to convince Dax to accept the inheritance and stay out of the books."

"And what about the widow, Caroline?" she said with a sidelong look toward the dining room.

"Divorced. Half owner. Knows nothing about the creative accounting."

"She could do time," Miss Dolly said. "She'd never survive."

"Even if Dax inherits, he's gonna find out about the books, eventually. And he's too honest to let it go on."

Dolly poured cream into her coffee, then stirred thoughtfully. "That would be bad for both of them."

"I agree. I think I've convinced Dax to accept it and let me run it for him."

Miss Dolly frowned. *"That* would be bad for *you.*"

"I'm just trying to buy some time. I'll figure out what to do about Vester Caine *after* I get Jack safe. Besides, I don't really see another option."

"Young people," Dolly said with a roll of her big eyes. "Do you really think if this got out among our own that there wouldn't be hell for Caine to pay? What's he got that makes him so scary?"

"Gee, I don't know. Automatic weapons and hit men and millions of dollars. And someone in his deep pockets from every branch of government from the cops to the White House. What've *we* got?"

"Brains," Miss Dolly said. She took a deep sip of her coffee, sighed in pleasure, and set the cup down again. "We're smarter than he is. And that's worth more than all the guns in Guatemala, baby." She winked. Then her expression returned to wide-eyed wonder in absolute sync with the bell over the front door jingling.

The upright women of Big Falls walked in. Sophie's and Emily's arms were loaded with gifts stacked up higher than their heads and over-stuffed plastic bags dangling from their wrists. Little Matilda Louise, Joey's little girl, was carrying presents too, and she was more adorable than Kendra could've imagined, all goldilocks curls and chubby cheeks. They didn't even notice Kendra and Dolly there in the back corner of the saloon as they all bumbled and stumbled across the bar into the dining room, laughing and talking all at the same time.

"Eat honey. I don't want Ned to be insulted."

"He doesn't have any money, Miss Dolly," Kendra said. She didn't know anything about Ned, so she was making it up from whole cloth. He might be a secret billionaire for all she knew.

"Maybe it's not his money I'm wanting a piece of," Miss Dolly replied with an innocent smile.

~

Ned came out the back door from The Long Branch's kitchen, and caught Dax's eye. Dax was standing beside a helium tank, inflating balloons for the party. Kendra said her sister would want lots of balloons. Some would float, while others would be filled with ordinary air so they could carpet the floor.

When he spotted Ned trying to get his attention, though, he handed the balloon in his hand off to Joey McIntyre, and headed across the lawn to where Ned stood a few yards away.

"How's it going, Ned?"

"It's not going," Ned replied. "It's not going at all. That's what I came out here to tell you."

"I don't think I understand."

"Dax, you're a friend. And I like you. But that woman in there is an angel and I can't bring myself to eavesdrop on her private conversation, even if it is for the good of the family."

Dax sighed and let his chin drop. "I'm kind of relieved, actually. I think it was a mistake to ask you to. I've been feeling guilty about it all morning. But just so we're clear, Ned, and for your own sake, I have to tell you, Kendra's no angel."

Ned smiled. "Who said anything about Kendra?"

Dax blinked. "You're talking about Miss Dolly?"

He rubbed his white and silver moustache, and lifted his bushy eyebrows. "That's a woman, right there. A real woman. I intend to woo her and I intend to win her. And reporting her private words to you is no way to begin a relationship."

"Um, Ned, you just met her. Unless I missed something."

"A man my age knows what he wants when he sees it, and doesn't waste time about going for it. Maybe you should take notes." Then he turned and headed back inside, whistling a happy tune, an unprecedented bounce in his step.

"Huh," Dax said. He rubbed the back of his neck as he watched Ned saunter back into the kitchen. As the door swung closed, the whistle became a song.

"What the—" Joey said, overhearing the gruff baritone. He came closer, a half-inflated pink balloon in his hand. "Is that *Ned? Singing?*"

"Sure is," Dax said. "I think he might be in love."
"Holy.... Miss Dolly?" Joe asked.
Dax nodded. "Looks like."
"Well, I'll be."

~

After breakfast, Kendra joined her sister's friends and relatives in the dining room. She set out centerpieces, straightened tablecloths, and arranged gifts on gift tables. Miss Dolly offered to help, too, but spent all her time flirting with Ned. Soon the room was ready, and all that was left to do was await the arrival of the guests of honor.

Rob brought Kiley to The Long Branch right on time. The big red velvet curtains were closed, but as soon as Rob's thundering pickup truck rolled in, Kendra peeked out between them. Everyone else bunched up, out of sight of the doorway so Kiley wouldn't see them as soon as she walked in. In spite of herself, Kendra had butterflies. She was excited about pulling off the surprise. How goofy was that?

They'd closed the saloon to the public for the shower, but Joey had thought to turn the OPEN sign back on just before Kiley was due to arrive. She and Rob walked in the saloon side, and they didn't seem to notice anything amiss. It wasn't empty. Several of the guests were scattered around like props, a few at tables, a few at the bar.

It was the most childish, ridiculous thing ever, Kendra thought, as others whispered and giggled like six-year-olds. And yet, there was a little girl inside her practically jumping up and down in delight as she backed away from the curtains and waited and listened to their footsteps coming across the hardwood floor.

Dax grabbed Kendra's hand, and she looked at his face and

he smiled. He was as excited as she was. God, what a pathetic pair of grownups they made.

Rob pulled the curtain open, and walked Kiley through, his arm around her shoulders. Two steps in everyone sprang out.

"Surprise!"

Kiley jumped backward and would've fallen over, if not for her husband's strong arm. "Holy smokes!" One hand on her chest, she blinked twice, then smiled broadly as she took in the decorations, streamers, balloons, and the big tables by the windows stacked up with more gifts than it should be able to hold, all of them wrapped in pastel, baby-themed paper and pink ribbons. Other presents were piled on the floor. A smaller table held three-tiers of cupcakes, white frosting with pink piping, all decked in purple and yellow Shasta daisies that looked too pretty to eat.

That Sunny had a knack.

"I can't believe this," Kiley said. Then, turning to look up at Rob, "Did you know about this?"

"I had an inkling," he said, and he sent an apologetic look at Dax. "You're not a very good liar. I did good, though, not letting on."

Kiley smiled. "I knew something was up when you insisted we come out for lunch even though I told you I had a backache. Usually, that gets me a massage, not a meal."

Rob grinned. "Your sister did this," he told her with a nod Kendra's way.

Kiley blinked as if he'd said the words in Swahili.

Kendra said, "All the work was done before I even got here, thanks to Sophie and Emily, Miss Vidalia, and Allie, and Sunny did the cupcakes."

"No, Kendra, you did a lot," Emily said. "Besides, we wouldn't have known to invite Miss Dolly without you." Her little girl Matilda was just then tugging Dolly by the hand.

"Miss Dolly's here?" Kiley said it in a soft whisper. And then she saw her, and Kendra watched, holding her breath for the reaction.

"Hello, Kiley, dear!" Dolly walked in staccato steps up to Kiley. She put both hands on her belly, patting it as if it was a puppy. "Hello, Diana! Ohhhh, you're gonna be so *precious*." Then she leaned in for a hug.

Kiley burst into tears and hugged her back. She sent Kendra a watery smile over Dolly's back.

Kendra almost sagged in relief.

"Let's get you off your feet, babe." Rob led the mom-to-be through the room to the big comfy chair they'd decorated just for her. She braced her hands on its arms, and lowered herself in, belly following like an attached beach ball. And she winced a little, and shifted position.

Kendra looked at her. "You okay?"

"Fine," she said. "Just a little bit pregnant. It's uncomfortable as hell, Kendra. I mean *all* the time."

"I bet."

"Thank you for this. You didn't have to." She held out her arms, and Kendra leaned in and hugged her, and whispered. "I didn't buy her any boy toys after all. I went with all things Wonder Woman instead."

Kiley laughed softly and let her go. "Good choice."

"Girl power," Kendra said, raising a fist. Then she had to move aside to let the rest of the guests take their turn greeting her twin. She went to Dax, because that was pretty much where she always went these days. "I think she really loves it," she told him.

"Was there any doubt?"

"Yeah. A lot."

"I'll tell Ned we're ready for the food." Dax leaned over and said it close to Kendra's ear, so close his warm breath tickled her there, and made her shiver against her will. His lips almost touched her earlobe. "You did really good. That was sweet, bringing Miss Dolly. You you're your sister happy." Then he turned to go.

Her cell phone vibrated in her pocket.

She pulled it out, saw the number and answered while walking quickly out of the big room. "Jack?" she whispered.

"Yeah, it's me."

"Thank God! When I told them it would be another week, I was afraid they'd—"

"Don't worry about your old man. When have I ever not been able to take care of myself?"

She blinked, not liking the sound of that as she found a quiet corner where she could talk. "They're not gonna wait, are they?"

"Everything's fine, at the moment," he said. "What's going on there? Sounds like you're having a party."

She lowered her head. "Baby shower for Kiley. I was hoping you'd be able to come."

"Your idea? You get strippers?"

She laughed softly, "Same wavelength, you and me."

"Always," Jack said. In her mind's eye, she saw the dimples she loved so much. If Vester Caine hurt her old man, he was going to *suffer*.

"There's a chance this could go sideways on me Kendra," he said. "I figure you should know that."

"It's not gonna go sideways. Don't say that."

"If it does, I don't want you feeling guilty. You did the best you could."

"Stop it, Jack."

"Yeah. I'm being melodramatic, right? Impending grandfatherhood will do that to a guy, I guess. Listen, get back to your sister. Worse comes to worse, you tell her…tell her I'm proud of the way she outfoxed her old man. Tell her I don't hold a grudge. And that I…you know."

"Love her."

"And you," he said. "And the kid. Diana. That's something, isn't it?"

"It's something, all right."

~

Jack hung up the landline phone.

"Anything new?" Phil was the one asking. Ace was too busy blowing his nose. Had been all through the phone call. All day, in fact. And for some reason, he'd stopped popping a Benadryl every few hours. He hadn't run out, there were still three boxes in the medicine cabinet.

"No change."

Phil shook his head. "Boss doesn't like it. He thinks your daughter's just stalling."

"Why the hell would she be stalling?"

"I don't know," Phil said. "Maybe to give whoever she's sending to save your sorry ass time to get here."

Jack said, "I thought you were the smart one. Look, this was my idea. I don't need rescuing."

Phil averted his eyes. "She doesn't know that."

"True enough, but that's why you agreed to let me talk to her. To reassure her I'm safe as long as she gets Russell to accept his damn inheritance. And that's exactly what she's doing."

Phil shrugged. Ace wiped his nose and tossed his tissue at the wastebasket. They were on the sofa, watching college football. The wastebasket was two feet further than he could reach from there, so he tossed each wadded-up bundle at it, and missed nine out of ten. Little white puffs surrounded the wastebasket like snotty snowballs.

"Boss says you're slick as a snail and twice as slimy," Phil said. "He thinks you might be running a game on him, instead of on her."

"Right," Jack said. "Look, he only pays me if I succeed. So

what am I conning him into? Putting me up here in this cable-free farmhouse with you two saints, straight through my favorite holiday? Boy, am I clever."

Ace laughed a little, and it turned into a cough.

Jack was lying, of course. Thanksgiving wasn't his favorite holiday. It used to be, though, back when the girls were just toddlers and their mother was still with them. Damn, that woman could roast a turkey that would tempt a vegan.

"What's going on, Phil?" Jack looked into his eyes and he didn't like what he saw. "Tell me the truth, come on. We're friends, aren't we?"

"Nothing's going on. Caine's just getting impatient." Again, he averted his eyes.

"Right. So why can't Ace take his Benadryl anymore?"

Ace said, "Makes me too sleepy. Mr. Caine's gonna bring some non-drowsy allergy tabs with him when he comes back tonight."

Phil glared at him, but by the time Ace noticed, he'd finished the revelation. He looked at Jack, and he knew that Jack was aware that his situation had changed.

"I'm not a guest here anymore, am I boys?"

"Sure you are, Jack," Phil said.

"Then I guess I'll go. Maybe I'll have better luck getting Dax Russell's cooperation myself." He got up, and moved toward the front door.

They both jumped up and stepped in front of him. He lowered his head. "Shit."

Ace was looking nervously from Phil to Jack and back again. Ace liked him.

"I probably oughtta thank you. I hated lying to my daughter. Even though I owed her one. Now I don't have to."

"It's not a big deal," Ace said. Phil elbowed him, but he went on anyway. "Nothing needs to change. We just can't let you leave."

"And Caine's coming back tonight?"

Ace nodded. Phil said nothing.

"He's gonna off me, and then he's gonna try to strong-arm Kendra himself." He sank down onto the sofa again, shaking his head. "Look, don't feel bad," he said. "I understand, Caine's a scary guy. You gotta do what you gotta do."

He pretended to watch the game for a few minutes, while his con-man's mind worked overtime to figure a way out of this mess. There was always a way out. Always. And he came up with a plan.

During a time out, he said, "You know, even on Death Row a guy gets to eat whatever he wants before he takes the long walk to nowhere. Can you do that much for me?"

Ace looked at Phil like a kid looking at a parent for permission.

Phil shrugged. "Sure," he said, sounding relieved, because honestly, they'd bonded, too, as much as Phil could bond with anybody. Sort of the way a killer whale bonds with its trainer before turning around and biting him in half. "If we have it here, it's all yours."

"I make the best chili in the country." Jack had pulled his plan together out of thin air, recalling what he'd seen in the kitchen while having free run of the place—a situation he figured was over with now. "I saw beans in the cabinets. Tomatoes, too—canned, not fresh but they'll do."

"We got some frozen peppers and onions, too," Ace said. "I'm real sorry this didn't go better, Jack."

"I'm sorry, too, pal. I'm sorry, too. Hey, before we cook, I need a drink. Is that still allowed?"

"Sure as hell is." Phil got up to pour.

"I gotta drain the snake. Be right back," Jack headed into the bathroom. He wasn't in there too long. He did what needed doing, quickly and efficiently. Then he washed his hands and headed back out.

Phil handed him a glass, then tinked his against it, and downed the whiskey in a single gulp. Jack sipped his and retreated to the kitchen with all the Benadryl from the bathroom cabinet in his pocket. Ace came with him, said he wanted to help, but it was clear he was supposed to be keeping an eye on Jack.

They chopped and sautéed frozen vegetables, and simmered tomatoes with beans and an butt load of spices. Jack cooked both ground beef and sausage. Then he mixed it all together and got it bubbling in a big pot on the stove.

He kept hoping Ace would get bored and leave the room, but he never did. Apparently, the guy was an assistant chef in the making. So Jack had to send him digging through the little pantry for another can of beans. "Pinto beans," he said. "Kidney beans are fine, but a can of pintos would really make this pop."

While Ace had his head in the floor to ceiling, curtain-draped pantry, Jack scooped out a bowl of the chili and hid it under a haphazardly tossed dishtowel. Then he added the final ingredient to the pot, the contents of all those Benadryl capsules, shaking the white powder from its toilet paper bundle.

He figured the meds would take a good hour to kick in. Maybe more, but the whiskey should speed things along. So all he had to do was feed them, and hope to God they passed out before their boss arrived to witness, or possibly conduct, his execution. Shouldn't be a problem at all.

CHAPTER EIGHT

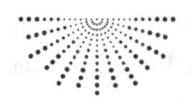

When the shower wound down, and most of the guests had left, Dax helped load mountains of gifts into the back of Rob's pickup. There was enough for ten babies piled in there, Kendra thought.

Ned and a couple of long-time waitresses were already busy taking down streamers. Joe's little girl, five-year-old Matilda was running around gathering up balloons. She could manage two at a time, kind of hugging them to her waist, one under each arm, but then she kept trying to go for three. She bent over a pink balloon, wiggled her fingers and twisted her hands, but she couldn't push her arms together around the balloons she already had. Little T-Rex, Kendra thought, and laughed out loud. Matilda pressed her arms harder, and both balloons sprang free. She dropped onto her backside on the floor. A blond curl landed across her face, and she blew it away with a pouty little puff.

Kendra experienced a warm wave of something in the middle of her chest, behind her ribcage and a little to the left. She looked at her sister, hadn't meant to, just did, and her eyes locked onto that bulging belly, and she thought of her niece being Matilda's age, that cute and that precocious and that pretty.

This thing was real. There was going to be a new person in her life. It was a big deal. Her eyes were getting all damp, stupid eyes, and when she dragged them off her sister's belly, she found Kiley looking right at her. She had an odd look on her face, like she was trying to interpret Kendra's interest in her belly.

Getting up with effort, Kiley came over. Kendra turned a little sideways to watch Joey, Matilda's father, handing her a giant trash bag.

The little girl's eyes lit up. "That's *brilliant!*" She shouted, springing upright and *at* him, like she'd been sitting on an airbag as it deployed. He totally knew it was coming, too, because he hunkered down and caught her for a great big hug. "Thanks, Daddy."

"Any time, Princess."

Matilda looked at the bag, a green one, then at the balloons all around the room. "I might need more than one bag."

"I think you can make due with one," her daddy said. "Maybe some of the other kids want to take some home. You think?"

"Okay." She ran off to fill her bag with balloons.

"She's cute, isn't she?" Kiley asked.

"If she was any cuter, I'd need insulin." Kendra softened the words with a smile. "Watching her made me think about Diana. And how big a deal this is." Her eyes were on her sister's bump again. And something pressed outward from one side, then receded, then gave three quick little jabs."

"Ow!" Kiley said.

"That's...that's unreal." Kendra put her hand on there to feel it. "It's like *Alien*."

"It is *not* like *Alien!*" Something poked outward slowly, making an odd and impossible lump. Kendra met Kiley's eyes, lifted her brows. "Okay, it's a *little* like *Alien*." She smiled. They both did. "I really want you to stay, Kendra." Kiley put her hand over the one on her belly.

Kendra lowered her head. "You want me to change, so I can stay." She already had changed. Sort of. But there was some stubborn streak preventing her from telling Kiley that. She wanted unconditional acceptance, she guessed.

"It's not so hard. And it feels wonderful not to have to deceive people all the time. You wouldn't believe the...the lightness of it. Never watching over your shoulder, worried about getting caught in a lie, never worried about getting caught, period."

She didn't doubt a word of it. It *did* feel good not having a cover to maintain. She hadn't realized how good until she'd had to maintain one again. And lie to Dax. And try to get him to do something he didn't want to do. And now she was racking her brain to figure a way to help him deal with Vester Caine once Jack was safe. There had to be a way to get Dax and Caroline out of this mess without one or both of them doing time.

She was also worried about Dax finding out the truth, Dax not finding out the truth, Dax going along with the plan, Dax refusing to go along with the plan, her father getting killed, her sister and niece getting in the way of this, and what the hell to do with Miss Dolly for the rest of the week.

Give me a minute, she thought, and I can make that list longer.

"Hey."

Kiley was searching her face when Kendra pulled her focus out of her own head. "Whatever it is," her sister asked, "can you do anything about it tonight?"

She thought and thought and thought. "I don't think so."

Matilda ran past them, her trash bag bulging with balloons and bouncing along behind her. She raced through the batwing doors and outside into the parking lot.

"If there's nothing you can do about it right now, why waste your time on it?" Kiley went on. "Let it go and relax."

"Where'd you get that crap? Oprah?"

"Allie. She reads a lot of self-help books." Kiley sighed and went on. "If you want to talk about anything, I'm here. Okay?"

Kendra's eyes were all hot and wet again. "God, you're so sappy now, you know that? What is that, a side effect of pregnancy?"

"Yes. Yes, it is."

Matilda came racing back through, trash bag empty now, and flying behind her like a banner.

Kiley laughed. "Thank you for the party, sis."

"Thank you for the niece."

Kiley hugged her and kissed her face. Then she joined her husband and headed out to their waiting truck.

Kendra walked outside behind them, Dax falling into step beside her, little Matilda racing behind them, her trash bag once again bulging.

They stepped aside to let Matilda and her bag of balloons pass, then followed her outside. She carried the bag right over to a pickup truck that had a mountain of balloons in its bed, climbed up onto the rear bumper and emptied her bag.

"Matilda what are you doing?" Emily, asked, trying to sound like a stern mommy, except for the laughter bubbling underneath her words.

"Daddy said I should make due with one bag, so..." She held up her hands, palms-up, on either side of her pretty face. Then she added, "I asked the other kids, Daddy. Nobody else wanted any."

Emily looked at Joey. Joey said, "She has not disobeyed me in any way. Followed my words to the letter. I said she could make due with one bag, and that's exactly what she did."

Jason came up, slapped Joe on the shoulder and said, "I've

got a tarp and some bungies. Let's secure your daughter's cargo, little brother.

Kendra stood there with Dax and waved goodbye as everyone left. The shower had gone really well. And now she was going to help with the cleanup, and make the best of the evening, because there was nothing else she could do tonight, anyway. Her sister had been right about that. So she pushed up her sleeves and started back to the dining room with the few remaining people. Ned was still there, and he and Miss Dolly were using cleanup time to continue talking, and laughing and touching every now and then. It was kind of sweet.

Everyone headed into the dining room. Kendra paused and glanced back at the bar. Might as well make clean-up as much fun as possible. She filled a glass with ice, then halfway with Coke, and then the rest of the way vodka, highest proof on the shelf. She dropped in a straw before moseying back into the dining room, where not a single balloon remained.

~

Dax could see that Kendra was tipsy. She was not drunk. He knew drunk from tipsy. She'd sneaked a couple of drinks when she thought he wasn't looking, probably because she knew he was on the wagon.

"It went really well, don't you think?" she asked.

"I think it was a huge hit," Dax said.

"I had a moment with Kiley, I think."

"I saw."

Everybody was gone, except for the two of them. The place was clean, chairs up on tables. Joey had been the last to leave, and he'd said, "I'll leave the back door open. Lock it up before you uh... whatever."

They were walking that way now, toward the back door.

Dax wasn't sure if Kendra was expecting him to leave and lock it behind him, or stay, and lock it from the inside.

He decided to find out, and locked the door, then looked at her, waiting for her to object. He did an internal happy dance when she didn't.

"Miss Dolly is sweet," he said, arm around her shoulders, walking them back through the kitchen, into the saloon, and around to the staircase.

"She's been flirting with Ned all night. I'm a little bit worried about him." She wrapped her arm around his waist as they climbed the stairs, let her head rest against his upper arm as they went up. "She's in the...family business."

"He'll be fine. He's ex-Navy." Then he thought a minute and smiled. "Besides, he's smitten. Well and truly smitten."

"Twitterpated," she said, laughing. "It *is* kind of sweet."

"You're kind of sweet, too," he said, and he turned her into his arms when they stopped outside her door. And then he kissed her, and as usual, common sense and rational thought left his mind. "You taste like vodka."

"I'm sorry. I'll brush my teeth."

"I like it." He kissed her again to prove it. He'd quit drinking, so this was as close as he was gonna get.

She kissed him back and pressed her key into his hand. He turned them sideways and maneuvered it blindly, jabbing and missing a few times before he manged to turn the key and open the door. They stumbled inside, still kissing, fell onto the bed still kissing, undressed each other, still kissing.

Sex with her always felt real. She didn't pretend, she didn't cover, she didn't hide. She let him see her soul when he made love to her. He stroked her secrets. He kissed her scars. He touched her fears, until she let them all go.

It had always seemed like she really meant it, when Kendra let him make love to her. And tonight, it felt like she meant it even more.

Later, when they collapsed in and around and against each other, breathless, plummeting to earth from heaven like the winking sparks of a fireworks display, he said, "I love you, you know."

And she said, "Yeah. I know."

He hadn't expected an *I love you, too*. He'd hoped, but he hadn't expected it. Probably just as well. If she said it now, before he told her what he'd decided, it might change anyway.

He sank back onto his pillows beside her, one hand behind his head, and watched her face. She was on her side facing him, knees bent and tipped over on top of his thigh, one bent arm across his chest, fingertips splayed over his heart. Maybe she was feeling it beat. It was beating fast. For her.

He looked right into her eyes. "I don't want to own a racetrack, Kendra. It's probably the thing I want least in the whole world."

She flinched as if something had stung her. And then her gaze seemed to be looking within. "Why not?" she asked. But he got the feeling it was filler, to give her mind time to write the rest of the script. All that connection, all that openness, was fading now. She was gathering her masks around her once again.

"On his deathbed, my father told me he'd have disinherited me if he'd known he was gonna die so soon. He'd intended to take care of it, just didn't get around to it. Who expects to die at sixty, you know?"

"Your father was an asshole."

"Yes. He was. But the fact remains, I don't want it, Kendra. He didn't want me to have it, and I can't swallow enough pride to take it on a technicality."

"But...but you could give the profits to your mother," she said.

"Mom and I had a heart-to-heart this morning. She feels the same way I do. She's a successful woman in her own right. She's got her boarding stable, and she does really well for herself. She's ready to let the track go, too. The SRA will pay market value if living heirs give it up."

Kendra swallowed hard. "So...then, you've decided?"

He nodded. "Yeah. I have a few technicalities to work out first, but yeah. Ultimately, we're letting it go."

"I think that's a mistake, Dax."

"Maybe. I just keep thinking how I'll feel when the newspapers run my name next to that track's name, and talk about the family legacy. Maybe they'll run my photo beside my old man's. It'll feel like a lie."

"Newspapers," she said softly. Then she sat up quick, hugged her knees to her chest, rested her chin on top of them. "And my shot at a new life? At a new career?"

"You already have a new career. Whether you keep it going, that's up to you. If we're gonna make this work, we have to give each other autonomy over our own lives."

"Autonomy, huh? So if I choose to go back to hustling fools?"

"Autonomy within reason."

"That's a double standard."

He nodded and sighed, sitting up beside her in the bed. "I only want to be with you if you can give it up for good, Kendra. I can be honest about that. Just tell me, do you only want to be with me if I own a racetrack?"

She looked at him for the first time, and he wanted to believe it was honesty he saw in her eyes. But with Kendra, you could never be sure. "My feelings for you have absolutely nothing to do with your father's racetrack. That's the truth, Dax."

He clasped her hands. "I want to build something of my own," he said. "No. I want *us* to build something of *our* own. Together."

She sighed, lowered her head, breaking eye contact.

"Do you want that, too?" he asked at length.

"I...I've got too much going on right now to figure out

something that deep on five minutes' notice, okay?" She dropped her face to her palms, pushed them up and back through her hair.

"That's fair," he said. "You're right. Take some time. I know this is a big change, Kendra, but I need your honesty. I need you to trust me. If we're gonna go forward together, I need there to be no secrets between us. That's crucial."

She lowered her eyes, hiding whatever was happening behind them. Again.

Sighing, he rolled out of the bed, stood up, and felt her looking at his naked body while he gathered up his clothes. "I'm gonna go."

"Stay," she said.

He turned around, his pants in his hand. "You need space to think about all this."

"I think better when I'm wrapped up in you. Stay, Dax. Really."

She could hurt him so bad if she wanted to. She was still keeping secrets from him. She might be sincere, or she might be a spider inviting the fly to a sleepover in her web. Man, he was some kind of idiot where this woman was concerned.

He dropped his pants on the floor and crawled back into her bed.

∾

The idea had come to Kendra full blown, as if left behind by the vodka's receding tide. She knew exactly what she had to do. As soon as Dax was snoring peacefully, she crept out of the bed, took his cell phone from the nightstand, and pressed his thumb to the home button to unlock it. Then she grabbed a robe and slipped out into the hallway, pulling the door closed behind her, but not letting it lock.

She walked a few feet down the hall in one direction, only to be brought up short by creaking and thumping and Miss Dolly saying, "Oh, Ned, oh, Ned!"

Kendra pivoted and tiptoed in the opposite direction as fast as she could go, clicking icons to keep the phone from locking up again on the way. In a quiet spot, she gave a gentle shudder to try to disengage the images of Dolly and Ned from her imagination as she surfed for the email address she needed.

~

Ace and Phil passed out before the end of the second football game. Phil was on the sofa, all cocked over to one side with his face on the arm and his mouth open. Ace had got up, staggered three steps, and then hit the floor like a sack of feed.

Jack searched them, found his phone in one of Ace's pockets —thank God. Ace wasn't bright enough to have removed the battery and tossed it someplace far away to prevent anyone tracking it, should they try. And Vester Caine hadn't thought to tell him to, because nobody can tell an idiot everything he needs to know. Some things were supposed to be obvious, like *always keep the barrel end of your gun pointed away from you*, and *don't stick Tic-Tacs up your nose*.

He pocketed his phone and Ace's pocket knife, then tossed Ace's and Phil's phones onto the coffee table. Just as he did, one of them vibrated. Curious, Jack glanced at it.

It was a text from Kendra, showing on the lock screen. When he'd called her the first time, it had been from that phone. And Caine had used it to text her as well. He was too smart to use his own. Records could be subpoenaed, after all. He could see the full content of the message on the lock screen.

It's done. Watch tomorrow's *Aurora Free Times* for proof.

Jack smiled from ear to ear, shaking his head. "Well, what do you know? She pulled it off." And here he'd been worrying she'd gone soft on the mark.

Too bad he was already this deep into his escape plan. There was an SUV in the driveway, the one they'd driven here in. He took the keys, and all the cash in both their wallets, which turned out to be over six-fifty. On the way to the front door, he snagged the whiskey and a handful of Vester's Cuban cigars. Then he put the cigars back and took the entire humidor. He could've looted the place for a lot more, but he figured he should *git while the gittin's* good, as his mother used to say.

She'd been a master, his mother. Reminded him a lot of Kendra.

He opened the front door, cringed at the loud creak it made when he did, and glanced back at the men sprawled in the living room.

"Goin' somewhere Jack?"

Jack's head snapped right just as Vester Caine got up from the porch swing, rising slow to his full height of about 6'4", big enough that he probably didn't even need the gun in his hand. He walked casually closer, flipped a light switch, and the porch was suddenly flooded and blinding. Looking down at the bottle Jack held by its neck, he shook his head, reached out with a free hand and took it while Jack was still trying to decide whether he could hit him upside the head with it and run.

Probably not worth the risk, what with the gun and all.

Caine twisted off the cap, took a long drink that made Jack's throat feel dry. Then he nodded at the fancy ass box cradled in Jack's other arm. "My cigars, too? Jackie, Jackie, Jackie."

Jack held the cigars out to the guy. "Here you go. All good. No need for the gun."

"Back inside." He waved with the barrel and Jack obeyed, reaching behind him to open the creaking screen door, and backing into the little farmhouse. He set the cigars on the table.

"Where are my boys, Jackie?"

Jack inclined his head. Caine looked through into the living room where the two were sacked out, one on a ratty sofa, and the other on the floor.

"You *killed* 'em?"

"*No!*" Jack all but shouted it. "No, no, they're just sleeping. I slipped 'em some Benadryl. They'll be fine. Might wake up with a little headache, but I bet Ace'll stop sniffling for a day or two."

"You're a little too clever for your own good, aren't you Jack?"

"That, I am," he said. "All that planning, all that cooking. And it turned out I didn't even need to escape. You'd have let me go in the morning anyway."

"Here it comes." Caine rolled his eyes. "What fairy tale you gonna spin for me now?"

"Check Phil's phone. Kendra texted it just as I was leaving."

The phone was on the coffee table, right in the open where Jack had left it, so Caine marched him in, then picked it up, keeping his gun on Jack. He tapped the phone so it came to life, and the notification appeared on the lock screen when he did. His eyebrows rose.

Jack thanked his stars for his girl and her skills. "Her timing stinks, but she got it done. I knew she would. Shit, if your guys hadn't already passed out I'd have called the whole thing off. I was just eager to get out of this—"

"Shup up, Jack." Caine tossed the phone on the table again. "She says watch the *Aurora Free Times* tomorrow morning for proof. That's how long you've got to live if this is bullshit. Now get your ass in the basement."

"Hell, not the basement. Look this thing's over. You won."

"I always win. And you'd better believe I'll be verifying every freaking story you or your damn kid tell me. You Kelloggs are a pack of manipulators and liars. Can't be trusted. So you want me to put a bullet in your head right now for all the trouble you've given me? Or are you gonna get your skinny ass into the basement?"

"Basement it is."

Caine followed him to the basement door. Jack opened it, flicked the light switch to the left, and felt a foot slam into the middle of his back. He pitched forward and tumbled down those rickety stairs like a boulder in an avalanche, breaking a couple risers on the way down. When he landed, he just lay there, not moving as pain screamed through every part of him.

The light flicked off, and the door slammed.

Jack wasn't sure, but he thought his arm was broken. He also thought Vester Caine was probably going to kill him in the morning, no matter what the newspaper had to say. And regardless, his million dollar payoff was not going to happen.

∼

Dax was an early riser by nature, but it was a ping from his cell that had stirred him awake this morning. He read the text. Then he rolled over in bed, and went real still and just looked at Kendra, lying there, her hair spread on the pillows, eyes closed, those long lashes on her cheeks. She was more beautiful than the sunlight kissing her skin. Waking up beside her was everything he wanted in life right then. It was perfect.

And it was a fantasy.

The text was from the accountant he had going over Aurora Downs' books. He said someone had been using the track to launder money. Dax knew you didn't launder money unless it was illegal money. Drug money, weapons-trade money, sex-trade money, something like that. The accountant sent a file. Dax viewed it. Saw it right away. The expenses were ten times what they should be, and many had, conveniently, been paid in cash. The accountant wanted to know what to do.

He replied, "Follow the money. Find out who." And then after an agonizing moment, he'd added, "Call if you find mention of Kendra Kellogg."

So he knew *what*. He just didn't know *who*. And he didn't know how Kendra was involved, or *if* she was involved, and he still had no idea how the hell to protect his mother.

He needed to get away from Kendra for a little while. He couldn't think straight when he was with her. She was like one of those hidden images you could only see when you lost your focus. He lost focus around her, and the illusion looked real.

Yeah. He decided to head home for a shower and fresh clothes, grab a bite and go to work. The day started early at Holiday Ranch.

He leaned in to kiss her cheek, and breathed her in. He hated to leave.

She stirred, smiled softly without opening her eyes.

"I've gotta go," he said. "I'll see you later, though. Okay?"

"Mmm-hmm."

She didn't even wake up all the way. He slipped out of bed, dressed quietly and headed for home. On the way, his phone chimed its incoming message signal, and he glanced at it. It was a text from the lawyer, with an image too small to make out.

He pulled into his driveway before taking a closer look.

AURORA SPRINGS' ONLY PRIVATE TRACK STAYS THAT WAY

Dax had to make the screen bigger to read the rest.

AURORA DOWNS' new owner Dax Russell is the late Nealand Russell's only son and heir. As his first order of business, Russell has appointed Kendra Kellogg manager. Background on Ms. Kellogg is a little hard to come by, but we'll know more right after the holiday, when *The Free Times* will have an exclusive interview with both her and Dax Russell about their plans for our beloved *Aurora Downs*.

Dax stared at the image filling his phone's screen for a long time and read it twice, before he realized that he was looking at a photo of the front page of the *Aurora Free Times*. He could make out the edge of the lawyer's coffee mug.

Did you do this?

He sighed at the phone, irritated, tapped in NO and hit send. Then he pocketed the thing, and wondered where the reporter had got his information. He thought about calling and asking the guy, but he probably wouldn't tell him. That was some kind of reporter code, wasn't it?

Besides he knew who'd done this. Kendra.

Others knew. Rob knew about Kendra's "brilliant idea" to manage the track. Dax had confided in him. And what Rob knew, Kiley knew. And it was common knowledge that whatever any member of the Brand-McIntyre clan knew, they all knew. They had a group text busier than the AP wire.

All those arguments came from the part of him that loved her. That was a really big part.

But his thinking mind wasn't dead yet. No one else had any reason to leak this lie to the press. He pulled into his driveway and shut the car off, then lowered his head to the steering wheel, not voluntarily. A wave of sadness washed over him, filled him, flooding in through a hole in his heart. It weakened his muscles. He felt heavy.

He pulled out his phone and saw three more texts from the lawyer. He didn't read them. He just typed "Don't tell Mom…" *Backspace, backspace, backspace.* "Don't tell Caroline and spoil her trip. I'm looking into this. Will get back to you."

He needed time to work through this, the grief of it. Because there was no question in his mind Kendra had tipped off the paper. He didn't know why, but why didn't matter. She was playing him again. He'd known it all along; he just hadn't wanted to accept it. She was involved, somehow, with whatever criminal had been using Aurora Downs to clean his dirty money. He didn't know who or how, but did it matter?

He'd walked right into this with his eyes wide open, told himself he could keep his heart out of it. But he hadn't.

The truth hurt more than he had ever imagined. It hurt like hot railroad spikes, driven straight through his heart.

And she was far, far crueler than he ever would've believed. Because she knew he loved her. And she'd played him anyway.

So he made his mind slow down a little, and he got out of the car, went inside, and tried to go through the motions of any other morning, hoping the emotional tsunami would wash back out to sea.

He backhanded wetness from his cheeks, made himself a single cup of coffee, spilled the cream he tried to add all over the table. His hands were shaking, he realized as he sat there, staring at the vibrations of the spoon he was holding.

He hadn't shaken this hard since he'd quit drinking.

Drinking—why did he have to think of drinking? The sensation and taste of whiskey splashed over his tongue, too real to be imaginary.

He got up, cleaned up the cream, put the carton back in the fridge. There was a muffin in there from Sunny's Place. That might soak up the lava bubbling in his stomach. So he took that to the table with him and ate it slowly, and drank the coffee, and waited for the killing-winds inside him to abate.

But they didn't. And he wondered if they ever would.

He rinsed his mug after the 2nd refill, cleaned up the muffin crumbs, and headed to the bathroom for a long hot shower.

An hour later, still feeling no relief, he drove down Main until he hit the Falls Road, and took that up into the woods and hills north of town. He headed back to the barely used dirt road that looped around at one end, and he drove over it once to check for hazards; boulders or limbs or potholes. It looked good. So he drove back to the beginning, lined up his wheels, and sat there. There was so much power under and around him that he felt its rumble, and revved the motor just a little, so the rumble became a roar. And then he released the clutch, stomped the gas and sent twin geysers of red dirt flying behind him before the tires caught and the Charger lunged forward. He gave it all he could, let off just before the curve, turned the wheel, gave it more again, and the car drifted around the loop almost sideways, then caught traction and sped back to the start again.

He wasn't timing himself, but he was sure he could do it faster.

～

～

Jack had fallen asleep, despite trying real hard not to, because he was afraid if he fell asleep after a concussion, he'd die. He knew that was an old wives' tale, but he was afraid all the same.

He wasn't used to being afraid. So far, he didn't like it much.

When he woke up, there was dim gray light coming through the skinny casement windows. The sun had not yet risen. He pushed himself up onto all fours, only one arm wasn't holding weight and screamed when he tried. So he got up on all threes. Moving hurt like a bitch. One knee was generating pulses of pain like a heartbeat and he quickly took his weight off it, and just sat on the floor, scooting back to a wall to lean against it. His head hurt, and his arm was like a bad toothache. The rest of his body seemed intact. He didn't seem to be bleeding anywhere.

He patted himself down, found his phone and the pocket knife, all that cash, and one lonely cigar. His head kept dropping to one side. His vision kept going dark. He yanked the phone out of his pocket, and looked down at its shattered screen. Hell.

But still…maybe. He opened the app, tapped the command. Then he got up on his toes and used the pocket knife to start working on the casement window. Those things were never installed worth a damn.

Kendra was pounding on Dax's door by 7:17 a.m. But she knew he wasn't there. She could feel it—a big pulsing emptiness that, now that she thought about it, always seemed to be around when he wasn't. The empty driveway further attested to his absence. That orange Charger didn't go anywhere without him, that was for sure.

Dammit, she needed to see him, make sure he hadn't caught on to her sleight of hand. If he had, she'd have to explain, but she would really prefer not to have to. Vester Caine and his henchmen would see the headline—she'd already forwarded them a direct link to the *Aurora Free Times* online edition. All she had to do was confirm that her father was free, out of harm's way, and then she'd tell Dax the truth.

She remembered, vaguely, that tender kiss this morning. His soft voice telling her he had to leave and that he'd see her later. She hadn't intended to let him go. She'd thought she would stick to him like glue this morning to make sure he didn't get wind of the headline in the Aurora Springs newspaper until she'd had the chance to come clean and explain. God, why had she let him go?

She headed out to her sister's place, because if Dax wasn't home or with her, then he must be out there with the horses.

When she got to Kiley's, she twisted her rearview mirror and looked at her reflection. A stranger looked back. Frightened eyes, all roiling with emotions, that kept filling with tears. Her lips kept quivering. Her heart was beating too fast.

She schooled her face not to look as guilty as she felt, and saw that the big barn door was open. Good. Maybe she wouldn't have to see her sister. Kiley could see right through her. She was the only one who could.

So she moseyed in through the open door, and then walked through the barn, which really wasn't a barn anymore. They'd converted it into a sprawling stable. It smelled of oats and molasses and horse. But it would always be the barn to her. The big barn. Kiley's artsy crafty trinket shop was the little barn. Both buildings used to be full of old junk and spiderwebs and mystery, and two little girls used to sneak out and climb through them in search of treasure, even though their father had told them not to.

So different now. No more secrets to uncover. They were open and clean and bright like Kiley's new life. Kendra, though, was still crawling through cobwebs and shadows. She went all the way through to the rear door that opened into the pasture and closed it behind her.

Rob was out there watching a horse run in circles around him. He held a rope that was attached to her harness, and turned with her as she trotted.

"Hey Rob," she called.

He glanced her way. "Morning, Kendra." He unclipped the lead and let the mare run off to do whatever horses did all day, then came to her. "Thank you for the shower. It was fantastic."

She nodded. "You're welcome. Sophie and Emily helped. So did your stepmother. Vidalia's something else, isn't she?"

"She sure is." He frowned, looking past her. "Kiley's in the house, if you wanted to uh—"

"No. No, I'll have to visit her later. Right now I'm just... I'm looking for Dax. He wasn't home so I thought he might be here."

"He texted me earlier, said he'd be late." Rob frowned. "Something wrong between you two?"

"Not as far as I know, but it's weird he's nowhere to be found."

"You call him?"

"I need to see him in person."

She could see Rob wrestling with whether he ought to ask why, so she said, "I'll find him. No problem. I'll visit Kiley another time. Bye." She turned and trotted to the barn, ducked behind the door again and ran back through it to her car.

She was a mile down the road when she saw him coming toward her. Didn't recognize the car at first. Dax's Charger was usually spotless, but today it wore such a thick layer of dust and dirt that it didn't even look orange anymore. More beige.

She pulled her car over onto the shoulder. He swung his around, and pulled it up behind hers. She sat there staring at him in the side mirror, her hands sweaty on the steering wheel. He didn't get out for a long moment. *He knows* rang through her head, and then repeated in the deep tones of a Gregorian chant. It was a death knell. *He knows. He knows. He knows. He knows.*

The filthy door opened. Dax got out.

Taking a deep breath, Kendra opened her door and got out, too. She started toward him. He came a few steps, then stopped and just stood there, looking at her. The wind messed with his hair, and the sun beamed, making the gold strands shimmer. But he wasn't smiling. His face was still, as if all the muscles had been paralyzed. As she got closer, she realized the pain only showed in his eyes. It was so intense, her first thought was that something must've happened to his mother. But right behind it came the truth. *Something happened to* him, *dumb ass. YOU.*

She moved closer, no longer doubting that he knew what she'd done. He'd probably seen the paper. She stopped with about a foot between his toes and hers, and looked him right in his wounded blue eyes, and tried to think of something to say.

"You leaked a lie to the *Aurora Free Times*."

"Yes, I did, but—"

"And they just took your word for it? Ran the story without even calling me to verify it?"

She pressed her lips, looked at her feet. "The email was from you. I sent it from your phone last night."

He just looked at her, his eyes moving all over her face, like he was trying to see the monster he knew she was, trying to see the visible proof of it.

"Before or after I told you I didn't want the damn track?"

"After."

"And after I told you seeing my name in the paper beside his was more than I could bear to think about?"

She nodded, lowering her eyes to the road at her feet. It was like that made it ten times worse for him. He tipped back his head, turned in a slow circle, and was blinking way too frequently when he faced her again. "Do you honestly think this is gonna force me to accept the inheritance? And even if it did, that I'd still put you in charge?"

"No. I didn't think any of that. I don't need you to accept the inheritance, Dax, I just need it to look like you did for a day or two."

He grimaced like he'd just caught a whiff of ripe limburger. "*What?*"

"Your father was laundering money through the track for Vester Caine—"

"Who the hell is Vester Caine?"

"He's a business man who imports heroin with his products. If the track goes to the SRA, a big spotlight shines on his deals and he's got more trouble than you can even imagine."

"If the track goes to me, I'll do the same thing."

"I know that and you know that, but Caine doesn't know that. He thinks he can buy anyone. And if he can't buy them, he'll threaten them or blackmail them or something."

"And you were putting me in his sites? Not to mention my mother, Kendra?"

"I didn't put you in his sites, Dax. You were already there."

"Bullshit. So how much?"

She shook her head, her explanation kept forming and dissipating inside her mind, but she'd better say something fast, or it would be too late. "How much what?"

"How much did he pay you to come down here and slide your sweet, sharp, deadly blade between my ribs? Again."

She stared into his eyes and knew she'd hurt him more than she had even realized. "My father's life."

He blinked.

"He's got Jack. If you don't inherit and call off the accountant, they're going to kill him."

He just stood there, staring at her like he wanted to be able to see through her. "Did you just make that up, just now? Cause that's pretty good."

"I recorded the conversations," she said, diving into her shoulder bag for her phone. "I saved every text."

"Or you made them up, you and some of your scam-artist pals. A little play acting for the idiot mark. What were you gonna do, take the job running Aurora Downs while secretly working for Caine? Or just rob the place dry and disappear? Maybe fake a second death and leave me thinking I'd lost the love of my life again?"

"Dax, no—"

"I need you to go," he said. "Get out of Big Falls."

"I can't." She held his gaze hard and shook her head harder. "I need to be here for my sister."

"Then I'll go."

"You can't. Rob needs you. The horses need you."

"His sister-in-law's a vet."

"He relies on you, Dax. He's your best friend. You can't just walk away. Who else is gonna pick up the slack once the baby comes? Who else will take care of things so he can stay with Kiley while it happens, and right after? There's no one else who knows horses like you do, no one else he'd trust with them."

He lowered his head. "I don't know why we're having this conversation. I don't need to explain my plans or reasons for making them to you. I'm done, Kendra."

"Dax, they threatened to kill my father. That's the truth."

"If that was ever a real risk, it's not anymore. Not if your con works, and let's face it, they always do."

He turned and started back for his car, but she ran around in front of him and stood there blocking his path. "I didn't have a choice."

"That sentence is never true. You *always* have a choice." He moved to walk around her.

She moved, too, her hands going to his shoulders in a knee-jerk movement fueled by panic. It flooded her with ice cold adrenaline and she couldn't think rationally. She just couldn't let him leave. The thought of him leaving this spot and then leaving town and just being gone from her life was absolute disaster to her.

"Please Dax. You don't have to inherit the damn thing. By the time the lawyers get here and you have your meeting, all this will be over with and you can tell them you don't want it, just like you planned to do. You didn't even need to know about this newspaper gag. Nothing's changed."

He looked down at her face and shook his head. "You still think this is about the track?" Then he sighed, long and heavy. "But I guess that's all it was ever about, isn't it? Good bye, Kendra."

He stepped around her again, turning her as he did, then opening his car door.

"Dax, I love you!" she shouted at his back.

He froze as he was about to get in. "Damn. I didn't think even you would stoop that low." Then he got in, pulled the door closed, backed around into the road, all without even looking at her again. And then he laid rubber and was gone

Kendra was dizzy and shaking and her heart was pounding so fast it was like the hooves of one of Rob's horses. She hadn't realized it until she'd said the words—words Dax obviously thought were lies. Maybe she'd thought they were, too, when they'd exploded from her chest without permission.

"I love you." She whispered them again and they felt just as shocking, just as impossible, and just as true.

She opened her mouth to try to catch her breath and couldn't, which made her breathe faster and press her hands to her chest. It felt all fluttery and stuttery and it hurt. It was a heart attack, she was sure of it.

A car went by. She heard it slow, and reverse, and then someone was beside her, holding one hand, putting an arm around her back. "Hang on, hang on, I can have you at Doc Sophie's in two minutes. Quicker than an ambulance. Come on, now."

She recognized the voice, the pear-shape even more. Allie Wakeland.

Her own car's door slammed. "I've got your keys. Your car will be fine." Then she was beside her again, helping her into the passenger seat of her vehicle. She slammed the door, and hurried around to get behind the wheel.

Kendra sat there with her hand on her chest, bent forward, gasping as Allie drove. She thought she would die before they made it to Doc Sophie's. She couldn't catch her breath. Her heart was racing like a runaway train. She was bouncing all over the seat, holding on for dear life. "You drive it...like you stole it," she managed between gasps.

"Just breathe nice and slow," Allie said as she sped back up Main then turned right. "In and out, nice and slow. You're safe. Everything's all right. We're already on Doc Sophie's road. See?"

"I think it's my heart," Kendra said. It was broken, that was what it was. Dax had broken it. She'd ruined everything with him and he'd left her and he was never coming back.

"Hey, hey hey, easy now, come on. Breathe."

"I can't get any air. I can't get any—"

The car stopped. Allie tapped the horn twice, then jumped out and came around. Kendra got out too, seeing the Big Falls Family Clinic sign on the lawn. Her legs were shaking so hard she could hardly stand on them. Allie pulled Kendra's arm around her shoulders, and helped her up the front steps and onto the porch of the big white Victorian. She tried not to lean on the small, pregnant woman too much. The door opened and a redhead came out to take over.

"I'll call her sister," Allie said.

She tried to say no, don't do that, but there wasn't enough air in the whole place to fill her lungs and consciousness seemed to be swimming away.

~

"Hey, sweet sister mine." Kiley's voice was soft, and so was the hand that stroked Kendra's hair up off her forehead. She was lying on a bed, but this wasn't a hospital. The windows were floor to ceiling, forming a curve in an alcove with a padded Victorian settee. A hanging ivy trailed all the way to the floor. Kiley was smiling down at her. "How do you feel?"

"Fine. I'm fine." She pushed herself up onto her elbows. "Where am I?"

"Sophie's clinic."

Right. Allie had brought her. She was at Doc Sophie's. "Did I have a heart attack? Shouldn't I be in a hospital?"

"It wasn't your heart, Kendra. Sophie says it was acute anxiety."

Kendra begged to differ, but as she looked around the room, she saw a little heart monitor blipping away, and she figured if it had been her heart, Doc Sophie would know it. Being a McIntyre, she'd probably had the best education there was.

"What happened this morning, Kendra? Rob said you came to the stable looking for Dax, then left without even coming in to say hello."

She looked sharply at her sister. Did she not know, then? Had Dax not told her?

No, of course he hadn't told her. Dax wouldn't tell a pregnant woman that her father might've been kidnapped and her sister was trying to scam him to save his life, unless she was lying about that. He probably thought she was.

"Kendra?" Kiley was waiting for an answer. "Did you find Dax? Did you guys have a fight?"

She nodded. "Yeah. I think he's...I think...I think it's over." Saying it out loud made her throat close, and she had to swallow hard before she could speak again. "He can never trust me again after what I did. I should've known that."

Kiley sighed heavily, and finally said, "You really...felt something for him this time, didn't you?"

"I did then, too. I always have. I just..." She shook her head rapidly, pushed herself the rest of the way up, and swung her legs off the bed. "I am who I am, you know? I'm not ashamed of it."

There was a tap on the door, and Sophie came in. "Hey girls. Kiley, can I have a minute with your sister?"

"Sure." Kiley leaned in and kissed her on the forehead. "I'll be right outside."

"Good. I'll need a ride back to my car."

"Your car's at The Long Branch." She left the room before Kendra could ask how it had got there.

Sophie said, "Do you wanna talk about it?"

"No."

"Okay." She sighed. "I can write a 'script for something calming, if you want."

"Do you think I need one? I mean, is this kind of thing likely to happen again?"

"Has it ever happened before?"

The day they took her dad away. The day they took Kiley away. They day Kendra had to move in with her first foster family. "Yeah. I guess it has."

"Then it could happen again. There are some tools for

coping with stress. Meditation. Yoga." She ignored Kendra's eye roll. "Also drink more water, eat more veggies, avoid alcohol." She shook a tiny brown bottle. "Take one of these only when nothing else works. Just one. It's fast-working."

"Thanks." She took the bottle, looked around for her purse.

"Your clothes and things are over there." Sophie pointed to a chair where her stuff was folded and stacked. It had floral upholstery and scrolled wooden arms and legs. "You can go ahead and get dressed now. Call me if you need me, okay? You have my number."

"I will. Thanks, Sophie."

Sophie turned for the door, then paused, and turned back. "You know, women need other women. I'm here for you if you ever want to talk."

Kendra lowered her head. "That's sweet of you. Thanks."

"You're welcome."

CHAPTER NINE

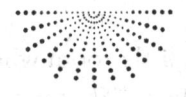

"Is she all right?"

Dax hated himself for rushing to Doc Sophie's with Kiley when she got the call. He'd been at the stable with Rob. Kiley had stopped on her way out to tell them that her friend Allie had found Kendra gasping and clutching her chest on the side of the road.

Right where he'd left her.

He shouldn't have left her there. If he'd caused something like this...

Doc Sophie came back into the waiting room, stethoscope around her neck, its business end in a pocket of her doctor-coat.

"She's fine. It wasn't her heart."

"Was she...faking it?" He stood there, kind of frozen, waiting for the ax to fall.

"You don't fake a heartrate of two-twen—I did *not* just divulge a patient's confidential stats." Then she frowned at him and tipped her head sideways. "Why do you ask? Has she been up to her old ways?"

Sophie had gone from medical professional to McIntyre in a dragonfly's heartbeat. She was protecting her family.

"No." It wasn't a lie. Kendra wasn't up to her old ways. She had all new ways this time around.

Sophie watched his face. He didn't know what she saw there. He didn't much care, he wasn't going to say anything that might lead to this kidnapping story reaching Kiley. Thinking her father was being held at gunpoint by killers could not be good for a woman as pregnant as she was. Besides, he didn't even know if it was true.

Kiley came out of the little room where they'd taken Kendra, an angry look on her face. "So now that I'm not afraid my sister's having a heart attack, you want to tell me what happened?" She was looking right at him, hands propped on her hips, chin jutting forward, but not as much as the belly.

"What do you mean? You're the one who got the phone call. Allie said—"

"I mean before."

Sophie put a hand on Kiley's shoulder, and tipped her head sideways.

"*What?*" Kiley snapped.

The doc gave her a look, and apparently Kiley understood it because she looked around the room and realized they were not alone. A handful of patients were waiting their turn. "Outside, Dax," Kiley said, pointing at the door.

He turned and went outside. Kiley spoke to Sophie, and then joined him, walking down three steps and over to where his car sat waiting. "I texted Rob to come pick me up," she said. "He'll be here in a minute, so talk fast. My sister shows up at the barn looking for you. Then she leaves. And then you arrive, and she's found having a full-blown panic attack a mile from my house right about the same time. So what happened?"

"We had a fight."

She grabbed his shirt when he started to turn away. "Tell me, Dax. She's my sister. What the hell did you do to her?"

Rob pulled in, braked and was out of the truck and at his

wife's side all in the same breath. "What's going on?" Hands on her shoulders, he pulled gently until she let go of Dax's shirt.

"They had a fight on the side of the road and he just *left* her there," she said, flicking a hand at Dax.

"I didn't know she was gonna have a meltdown. How could I know?"

"You don't just break up with someone and leave them on the side of the road—"

"She had her car, Kiley. Don't make it sound like that. And I didn't break up with her, because we were never together."

"Yes, you were."

"We were... It wasn't..." He lowered his head. "I don't know what it was. I don't know what happened. I'm sorry. Rob, I'm sorry. The last thing I want to do is upset Kiley--"

"I know, buddy. I know." Then he turned to his wife. "I don't think Dax is the bad guy, here, hon."

"Hello? She had a panic attack! Do you know how many times my sister has *ever* had a panic attack in our entire lives?" She uncurled fingers from a shaking fist to count them off. "When our father went to prison. When we were taken from our home by social workers. And when they split us up. That's it, Dax. So you tell me, you tell me what happened between you that was on a scale that huge? And how did you think it was okay to devastate her and then just walk away? Huh?"

He just blinked, because he didn't know what to say. "I... I gotta go. She's okay, though, right? You guys... you've got her?"

"Of course we've got her."

God, it hurt to have Kiley talk to him like that. They were friends.

"Go," Rob told him. "I've got 'em both. I'll call you later." His eyes were sympathetic.

Dax went to his Charger and fired it up.

∼

If Kendra hadn't been getting hit on by hot-rodders every time she pulled her little red 'Vette in for gas, or food, or a restroom all the way from the east coast to Oklahoma, she wouldn't have started noticing how they all sounded. But she *had* noticed. Hot rods didn't sound like other cars. And they didn't sound like each other, either.

She'd noticed right away the particular way Dax's Charger sounded. So, when it started up outside, she knew it was him. She went to the window, still pulling on her jeans, and moved the curtain with one hand in time to see him driving away, down the road. He'd been there, at the Sophie's office.

It was a little flicker of light in the dark hole that had opened in her chest. Maybe he still gave a damn. Maybe she could still make it up to him.

She took a deep breath and buttoned her jeans. Then she gathered up her bag and headed back out into the waiting room, just as Kiley and Rob came in from outside. Kiley came right to her, took her arm like she needed help.

"I'm good, sis," Kendra said. "If anything, *I* should be helping *you* to the car."

"I think you should come and stay with us, Kendra," she said. "I want to keep an eye on you."

"No." She smiled at her sister and shook her head. "I like my space. You know that."

"I know that," Kiley agreed. "But...just for tonight?"

"I'm okay, I promise." Jack would be calling just as soon as he possibly could, to let her know he'd been released. If he'd been released. He might've called already, if the damn headline had worked. She couldn't even imagine taking that call with Kiley nearby and not giving something away. She couldn't even check her phone until she got somewhere private.

Kiley said, "If you want to talk about...whatever happened between you and Dax—"

"It's not my style to slobber all over my sister every time I get my nose broken. I'm all right. But I do need to be alone to... process some things."

"I get that." Kiley sighed, nodded at the truck. "We'll drive you back to The Long Branch, then."

So they dropped her off in the parking lot and drove away, and she walked around back to use the outdoor stairs because she wasn't in the mood to make small talk with whoever happened to be inside the saloon. She made it all the way to her room, closed the door behind her, and finally pulled out her phone to check for anything from Jack.

An alert was flashing on the lock screen.

PHONE FINDER ACTIVATED

∼

Jack woke up so cold his teeth were chattering, and had no idea where he was or how he'd... Right, right. Vester Caine, the farmhouse, his body pounding down those basement stairs. He sat up slow as it all came back to him. It was daylight. He was on the ground, in a thin patch of scrawny trees. Saplings. His arm was throbbing and his head hurt. He remembered prying the casement window out, and crawling through the hole it left in the wee hours before dawn. He thought it a pretty good bet that it wouldn't matter what showed up in the *Aurora Free Times*. He'd pissed off Vester Caine, drugged his men, and tried to steal his cigars. He was going to be shot if he didn't get out. So he got out.

He wondered how far he'd made it before he'd passed out. A mile? More?

Somewhere, a door slammed. "Move it!" a deep voice roared. "Find that sneaky sonofabitch!"

Okay, he hadn't made it a mile. He hadn't even made it a hundred feet. When he looked in the direction that voice—Caine's voice—had come from, he had a clear view of the old farmhouse with its peeling white paint and weed-patch border. Ace and Phil were heading into the woods, in two directions. Caine was heading in another. None of them were coming directly toward him.

He got to his feet, but stayed in a low crouch, keeping them in sight, moving to the furthest spot from them, around behind the farmhouse. He wasn't going to get away from them. Not on foot, he wasn't. His grave would be a shallow one in this scrublot if he didn't put some distance between him and them fast.

He checked his pockets again, found his phone with the shattered screen. He'd known that already. He'd tried to send a distress call, hadn't he?

No time. Not now. He might have a chance, and it might be his last one. He crept to the edge of the trees, right up to the waist-high weeds that had once been the farmhouse's back yard. He could hear Caine and Phil and Ace crashing through the woods, looking for him.

Fine. He had one chance, the way he saw it. If it didn't work, he was dead, but he was dead if he didn't try it too. He dashed through the weeds to the back door. It was unlocked, the first piece of good luck he'd had so far. He opened it and ducked inside, racing through that place like his feet were on fire. Kitchen. Nothing. Dining room, nothing but the humidor and the whiskey. Living room. Score. A set of keys on a Cadillac keyring right on the makeshift coffee table. He grabbed them. Then he ran back through the dining room and paused.

Yeah, why not?

He grabbed the whiskey and cigars, and headed back through the kitchen, and out the back door again. He took time to listen for them. He couldn't hear much, which probably meant they'd gone farther away. So he crept around the house, and quiet as a mouse, put his treasures into the Caddy, closed the door so softly it didn't even latch. Then he yanked his pocket knife out and went to the SUV that belonged to either Phil or Ace. Probably Phil. He jabbed the knife into three tires, stabbing into the sidewall and ripping forward to ensure they'd go flat faster. As he got to the fourth tire, front driver's side, he saw through the window that the keys were in the switch. Well, hell. He took them and ran back to the Caddy.

They were gonna hear him start the motor. There was no question about it. And there was only one road. He held his breath, cranked the key, slammed the car into gear and stomped it. The back tires spewed dirt and gravel, then caught. He took off like the very devil was after him, keeping his head low in case they came out of those trees shooting.

But they never did.

∼

"Oh, God, oh God, oh God," Kendra whispered, pushing back her hair with one hand, tapping the phone locator app with the other. Jack must've activated his, and if he had, that meant he was in trouble.

He was always about the backup plans, and he loved technology. Said it had revolutionized the business. She was grateful for that as she read the notification on her screen.

PHONE FINDER has been activated for one of the devices on your account. That device has been located.

She could hear her father's voice just as clearly as if he was standing there beside her.

"Old-school scammers have to adapt or go extinct. Tech is either an opportunity to con better than ever before, or the end of your career. You get to choose. Me? I'm gonna ride the wave."

Jack Kellogg, con-man philosopher.

She tapped the "Send to Map" button, and it opened, showing a road map with a pulsing blue dot on it, and a "Start" button for turn-by-turn driving directions.

Her father was in Oklahoma. And not very far away, either. An hour, in the 'Vette.

She pocketed the phone and yanked opened the closet to pull out a small hard-shell case. It was ivory-colored with lavender blossoms all over it and looked about big enough to serve as a makeup bag. It was a case she'd hoped never to have to open, but she had to now. She took out her handgun. It was shiny silver, brand new. She'd never even fired the thing, but she knew how. Jack made sure his daughters knew how to handle firearms, just in case. He hated the things, said any con who had to resort to violence, much less gun violence, shouldn't be in the game. But he also believed that in their business, it was better to have one and know how to use it, than not. There was no telling how mad a mark might get.

The gun, a 9-millimeter Ruger, had been a Christmas present from Jack two years ago. She checked that the safety was on and the barrel empty, then filled the magazine. She was already wearing jeans, but her blouse had to go. It was low-cut and sexy, chosen with Dax on her mind. She took it off and pulled on a T-shit that fit snug and moved easy. Her stilettos would be useless in a fight, so she traded them for soft socks and lightweight black hiking shoes. She put the black leather jacket back on, shoved the gun into her right pocket, spare clip in her left. She grabbed her purse off the bed where she'd thrown it, and started back outside, but her phone rang.

She was so wrought up, she answered it without looking first. "Jack?"

"No, it's me," Dax said.

"Oh." She sighed, disappointed to her bones. "I can't talk now, Dax, I—"

"What's going on? You sound upset."

"Having your father threatened by killers is upsetting. Sue me." She went outside and down the back stairs.

"Shouldn't he be free by now? Isn't that what your ruse with the newspaper was supposed to accomplish?"

"Yes, it is, and no, he isn't. I don't—" Her voice broke. Her eyes burned. She hurried around the building to where someone had parked her 'Vette, unlocked it. "I don't know if he's okay. I don't know if he's already…"

"You haven't heard from him," he said.

"He activated a phone location app. Hours ago, and I had the damn sound off because I was all wrapped up in…" You, was the word she didn't say. "He wouldn't have done that if he wasn't in trouble."

"So, wait, you know where he is, then."

"I know where his phone is."

"Okay, good. Then we'll go—"

"I'm already going." She put him on speaker, pulled-out the car's ashtray drawer, and used it as a phone holder.

"Alone? Kendra, wait for me. I'm on my way."

She put the car into reverse and backed out of the spot. "I don't have time to wait. Any second might be one second too long, Dax." She shifted and drove out of the parking lot and up the curved drive to the road. She hit the pavement, and his Charger skidded to a stop just before hitting her.

"I'm already here," he said.

She never slowed down. If anything she went faster. But he followed. And the call was still connected. She kept looking into the rearview mirror. He kept on coming.

She said, "I need you to stop, Dax. Go back to Big Falls."

"I can't."

"Why the hell not?"

He hesitated for long seconds as she caught gears and picked up speed. "I'm just doing what I feel I have to do, okay? So where are you going? Where does this app thing say his phone is?"

"About eighty miles east. Hang on." She glanced at the phone while driving, which was stupid, but she had to see the Share button to tap it. So she did, briefly, and the app texted Dax the coordinates. "Just in case you can't keep up."

"You're kidding, right?"

Kiley smiled very slightly. She'd given in too easily, and she knew it. She didn't want her kind of trouble touching Dax any more than it already had. But the truth was, she was afraid she was going to walk into some cheap motel room or abandoned hovel and find her father with a neat round bullet hole his forehead. The truth was, she felt better knowing Dax was right behind her. She'd feel better yet if he was in the car beside her, but she hadn't dared take the time to switch cars.

She looked in the rearview mirror, saw him behind her. It felt good. "Thanks, Dax."

"You're welcome."

She sniffled and swallowed, a giant wave of relief crashing over her like a breaker over a dry and thirsty shore. And just as quickly it receded and something else came. Something cold and dark. She still had ice water running up and down her spine. Jack would have to be facing certain death to send his location and scare her this badly. And it had already been hours. She'd had her stupid fight with Dax and subsequent panic attack like an amateur. Caring about people was the stupidest thing a con could do.

And she'd done it. She'd done it in spades. She loved her sister more than she'd ever realized, and she loved Kiley's cow-eyed husband too. She loved little Diana more than words could say and she hadn't even met her yet.

She loved Dax Russell.

She did. She loved him. Good God, there was no hope for her now.

She pressed harder on the gas and she drove.

∼

The pulsing blue dot led them to a cheap motel called the Roadside Lodge. It had two long narrow buildings with rooms, each with a front door and a back door, and parking spots outside both. The only car there was a sweet-ass Caddy parked behind Room 2. She skidded the 'Vette to a halt right beside it, dove out of the car and lunged toward the door as Dax's Charger stopped behind her, making way too much noise. He was out of it before the engine even had time to quit.

"Kendra, wait!"

For a big guy, he sure could move fast. He was behind her clasping her shoulders before she even made it to the white door with the tacky metallic gold trim and a 2 stenciled dead center. The owners hadn't even sprung for the metal kind that you had to attach. Just paint and a stencil. The gold had bled onto the white. She wanted to slam that ugly door off its hinges and go get her father. But Dax squeezed gently.

"Just in case someone's in there with him," he said soft, near her ear. "Let's just take a peek before we go bustin' in."

Her hand clenched and unclenched on the gun in her pocket. Dax's nearness couldn't break the hold fear had on her. If Vester Caine had hurt Jack—She slid her fingertip back and forth over the safety catch. She'd never thought she had it in her to shoot someone, but now she wondered if maybe she did.

"Come on." Moving beside her, Dax let one hand rest on her opposite hip, and crouched low as they crept to the small window. They peered inside through the bottom edge of the beige curtains.

Jack Kellogg was sitting up on the bed, one arm behind his head, watching TV. He had a motel issue water glass half-full of amber liquid in his hand and a cigar clenched in his teeth. It was fat and brown and sending a ribbon of gray smoke to the ceiling where it became a cloud. She could smell it from where she was. A bottle of whiskey stood on the nightstand beside a wad of cash. Jack smiled at something on the TV while its light and shadows shifted on his face.

"That son of a—" Kendra lunged away from the window and pounded on the ugly door beside it. "Jack! It's Kendra. Open up!"

There was shuffling, swearing, and then Jack opened up the door, still hopping to get his pants up over his boxers. "Kendra! Damn I'm glad to see you." He patted her shoulder in lieu of a hug and gave her his best fake smile, which wasn't good enough to fool her. "Good news, little girl. I got away."

She punched him right in the face. His nose cracked and his body turned sideways from the force of the blow. The impact recoiled through her fisted hand and up her arm.

Jack stumbled backwards, and bent over, holding his nose with one hand. There was blood. "You better start explaining fast, Jack or I swear to God—"

"You're reading this all wrong, kiddo." The words were muffled by his hand. He lifted his head but didn't look her in the eye. "I fed the two thugs chili-con-Benadryl and they went out like lights, but when I headed out the door, there was Vester Caine himself on his way in."

"Save the bullshit," she said. "You broke the code, Jack. You don't game family."

"Uh, yeah, your sister broke it first. And you helped."

She felt her eyes widen.

"Yeah, I know you helped her pull one over on the old man. But that's beside the point." He held up the arm that wasn't busy with his nose. The entire forearm was purple and brown. "Caine threw me into the basement, broke my freakin' arm, I think. Scrambled my brain a little bit too."

She wouldn't put it past him to cause his own injuries. She'd seen him do it before, to lend credence to a story. But maybe not this bad. His arm looked damn awful.

Dax said, "Your nose is bleeding, Jack."

"I'm aware of that, Dax."

Kendra stomped past her father and into the bathroom, where she cranked on the cold water and soaked a couple of washcloths. "Keep talking."

"Caine was gonna shoot me right there, when he saw his guys out cold like that. Would have, if not for you, Kendra. Your text saved my ass, made him decide to keep me alive until morning."

She came out of the bathroom while he was still talking, handed him an ice cold, wet cloth and he pressed it to his bleeding nose.

Dax was looking at her, a question in his eyes.

"I texted the kidnappers that there would be proof I'd complied with their demands in the morning edition of the *Free Times*."

Dax lowered his chin, aimed his eyes past his own left shoulder, like he couldn't look at her. Like the reminder of her deception caused him physical pain.

"I reclaimed my phone and a pocket knife during my first escape attempt. Idiot didn't bother to search me before kicking me ass over elbow down that flight of stairs. I didn't remember if I'd managed to activate that phone locator app or not before I passed out. Didn't know if it would even work. Screen was shattered. Apparently, it did."

"And then what?"

"I passed out for a while. When I came to, I pried out a casement window and ran for my life. Wasn't sure if that newspaper text was a ruse or not, and I was pretty sure Caine was gonna off me either way, so I got my ass outta there. Passed out in the woods before I got very far."

"Uh-huh." She was eying the room, the whiskey, the cigars, the other set of keys on the nightstand. "And you what, went shopping while running for your life?"

"Slipped back inside when they started searching the woods

for me. Took the keys to the only other vehicle, slashed its tires, and helped myself to some cash, whiskey and cigars for my trouble. Took Caine's car, too." He sounded proud of it. "He's gonna realize he messed with the wrong guy."

"He's gonna be furious. He's not gonna let this go, Jack."

"I don't plan to be anyplace he can find me," he said. "Matter of fact, I was just about to leave for parts unknown." He sent her a quick look. "I was gonna call you first, tell you goodbye, of course."

"That's real thoughtful of you, Jack. So you just hurl a hornet's nest at Kiley and me—at your baby granddaughter—and then run like hell. That's *real* nice."

"What do you…?" But he knew. She saw when it dawned on his face.

"That's right, Jack. If Caine can't find you, who the hell do you think he's gonna take it out on?"

A phone rang. Jack answered it.

"Put it on speaker!" Kendra's voice came out so hard and commanding she didn't even recognize it. Then she lunged at her father, snatched the phone from his hand, and tapped the speaker icon herself. The glass screen was shattered, just like he'd said.

"Nice job getting Russell to accept the track and call off the snooping CPA," it said. "Needless to say, though, you are not getting paid. You broke the deal."

Paid? Kiley shot her father a look of disbelief, her brain going into overdrive.

"Meanwhile, I have your daughter. Didn't know you had a grandkid on the way. I'd say

congratulations, but it might be premature."

Kendra whispered Kiley's name. It felt like all the blood in her body turned to ice and fell to her feet. She was dizzy. Jack's face went white. Every bit of swagger and cockiness just dissolved.

Dax moved closer and leaned in. "This is Dax Russell. I assume I'm talking to Vester Caine."

"You assume right."

"Mr. Caine. You can do whatever the hell you want with the track. You can run it, for all I care. Just don't hurt Kiley."

"That's real nice of you, Mr. Russell, but with all the trouble you and Jack were making for me, I went ahead and made other arrangements for my needs. You can shove your damn racetrack. Turn your back on a fucking fortune cause you're mad at Daddy. Who does that? Listen, I don't want your track. I don't need it anymore. All I want right now is Jack Kellogg and if I don't get him, I'm gonna kill his daughter and his grandkid."

Jack reached out and snatched the phone. "It's Jack. Let me talk to her."

"You can talk to her when you keep the bargain."

"If I don't hear her voice, there's not gonna *be* a bargain."

"What the hell are you doing?" Kendra yanked the phone from him and turned away.

"Don't listen to him. I'll bring him to you myself, just… are you there? Hello? Hello?"

He was gone.

Kendra lifted her stricken gaze to Dax's, then turned toward her old man. "Are you *trying* to get my sister killed?"

"He's not gonna hurt your sister," Jack said.

She stood there blinking at him, wishing she could shoot him and wondering why she didn't. "You hate her for betraying you."

"This hasn't got anything to do with that." Jack grabbed the Caddy keys off the dresser, then started gathering up all the rest as well. It was more than he could carry in one arm, the humidor, the bottle.

"What did he mean, about you not getting paid?"

"No idea."

She blinked at him as the pieces clicked together in her

mind. "You did this. You did all of this, didn't you? You weren't kidnapped at all. You made a deal with Caine. You tricked me into conning Dax again, when you knew...you knew..."

"What did I know?"

She shook her head. "You knew I couldn't do it anymore. That the last time...changed me."

"I thought it might help you get your edge back. I was doing you a favor. You'd be thanking me if it had worked." He shrugged. "But you were too slow, Caine got impatient, and everything went sideways. I'm lucky to be alive."

"I can't believe you. I can't believe I left my sister to try to save your worthless ass. I can't believe I ruined the only good thing in my life to try to save yours, when it wasn't even real."

"You're right. I played you," he admitted. "Kind of makes us even, doesn't it?"

"That you can run out on us, after you've caused so much harm—how can you do that?"

His back was toward her, but he'd gone still. He dropped the whiskey and the humidor onto the bed. "I'm not running out. I'm coming with you to save Kiley." Then he turned slowly, blinking like a blind man when light somehow gets through. "You really think I'd run out on my own kids, Kendra? I mean, I was going to leave, yeah, but I hadn't thought it through far enough. I would have, before I got very far. I'd have come back. How can you think otherwise? Have I been that bad a father?"

"Yeah. You have. Come on, Dax." She was out the door a second later, and striding through the parking lot purposefully. Then she got into her Corvette, and started it up.

Dax stood beside her car, so she didn't shut the door. "If he's coming, he should ride with you," she said. "God only knows what kind of tracking that asshole Caine has on his Caddy."

"Okay."

She looked up at him. "I'm sorry, Dax. I thought I had no

choice, and it was all for nothing, and I fell for it like a rookie. And I'm sorry."

He said, "I am too, Kendra."

∼

"This is it," Kiley's kidnapper said after forcing her to hike what felt like miles uphill, through dense woods and undergrowth. "I told you it wasn't far."

"It was far for me." She wrapped her arms around her belly, as if she could protect the baby. They had reached a shack that looked like it was on the verge of falling down.

There were two men. The one in charge was a tall man, and way too well dressed for hiking through the woods. His suit was shiny. He had dark hair, male pattern baldness, a pock-marked face, and an oddly high-pitched voice. There was another guy with him, a big guy with carrot colored hair and freckles and eyes as cold and heartless as marbles. His name was Phil. The boss was "Mr. Caine." At least that was how they addressed each other.

They didn't speak to her much at all, except to give orders. She'd asked over and over what this was all about, but they wouldn't say.

"Is that an outhouse, over there?" she asked, pointing at the sturdiest piece of construction in sight.

"Yeah," Phil said.

"I need it."

"No." That was Caine, the boss.

"I'm nine months pregnant. There's an eight-pound baby sitting on top of my bladder. If I don't pee in the outhouse, I'm going pee in my pants. You want to smell *that* the whole time we're here?"

Mr. Caine studied her for a moment. "Go ahead but uh— don't try anything."

She strode to the outhouse, opened its door and poked her head inside. Quick as a minute, she snapped off her smart watch and tucked it behind a board. That way, it could keep beaming her location until help arrived. If these two douchebags found it, they'd smash it.

Then she backed out again. She hadn't even stepped all the way in. "I'll just go behind a tree or something. I think there are things nesting in here."

"Fine, just don't try anything funny."

"What am I gonna try? Sprinting through a forest, ten miles from anywhere? Idiot."

Only, she wasn't ten miles from anywhere. She'd been trying to pay attention to the landscape as they'd hiked, and she thought she was about a mile from the Falls, and Edie Brand's place wasn't far past them. She had that giant dog, Sally, too. Even if no one was home, Sally would protect her.

But Rob would be coming or her. These animals hadn't hurt her yet. Maybe they didn't intend to. And Rob would think to trace the watch. He'd be here.

So she didn't try anything. She went behind a tree, and peed, and found a tissue in her pocket to use. She was pretty sure the muscle, Phil, could see her the whole time, and she didn't give two nickels about that. He had his gun out, like he'd shoot her if she took off through the woods. So she stroked her belly as she walked back toward him, and sang a lullaby to her baby, and looked him right in his cold marble eyes.

He looked away.

CHAPTER TEN

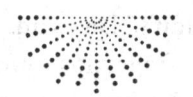

Rob had found Kiley's Jeep in a ditch about a mile from their home. That's where everyone was when Kendra arrived. Rob, Jason, Joe and Emily, Doc Sophie and Darryl, and a couple of local cops were already there. Kendra got out of her car and ran toward her sister's little red Wrangler. It rested at a cockeyed angel, and its passenger side front fender was crunched inward.

It hit her hard, seeing that.

Dax put his arm around her, squeezed her like he knew. Rob came to her other side. Kiley had texted him verbatim, the phone call from Vester Caine.

"She had breakfast at the diner with Vidalia and Miss Dolly. It's not that long between when she left them, and when you texted me, so he can't have taken her far. Jimmy and the State Police have roadblocks up in a thirty-mile radius."

Police chief Jim Corona said, "We also have a lot of questions for you, Jack Kellogg. What the hell is this about?" Jim was married to one of Rob's stepsisters, the sweet, shy one with the daycare business.

"Let's focus on getting my daughter home, and then we can talk all you want," Jack said.

Kendra couldn't take her eyes off Kiley's car. "Is there—"

"No blood," Rob said. "No sign she was hurt. But the airbag went off."

"That could've hurt the baby, couldn't it?" Her heart was breaking.

"More likely that it didn't," Dax said.

Kendra pressed her fingertips into her forehead. "Okay, okay, where could he take her?" She turned in a slow circle. "Where *would* he take her? The highway's that way."

"Blocked at the next exits in both directions," the chief said. "Before he had time to get that far, too."

Kendra forced herself to look away from the Jeep. "Can we track her phone?"

"We're already tracking it."

The Big Falls cop was good. Professional, competent. Seeing a good cop in uniform had never felt reassuring to Kendra before, but it did then.

He went on. "But a man like Caine probably knew enough to toss it. We have helicopters on the way for an air search, as well. We're going to find her. And we'll do it soon."

Man, Kendra thought, her sister sure had herself well-connected these days. If anyone could get her back, these people could. She didn't know why she felt so sure about that. It was kind of a deep, inner knowing.

Several of their phones chirped, beeped, buzzed, or jingled.

"Group loop!" Emily shouted.

They all picked up. Dax and Kendra, whose phones hadn't made a peep, had to lean over Chief Jimmy to see his. Jack did the same with Rob, which was brave, because Rob would punch him in the face if he knew the whole story.

The text message was two words.

Banana hammock.

"What the—"

"It's our old code!" Kendra wanted to crawl through one of those phones to her sister. "When we were younger, if we needed rescuing from a bad date, we'd text Banana Hammock, and the other would call with a fake emergency or come and get us." She gazed down at the screen. "Could she still have her phone?"

"No, no look!" That was Emily. She pointed at the tiny words in pale gray that appeared above the text. "Sent from Kiley's watch,'" she read aloud.

"She's wearing her watch!" Rob shouted. Jack wasn't beside him anymore.

Kendra frowned, looking around for him. Where the hell did he go?

"We can track her from my phone," Rob said. He reached to his pocket. "Where the hell is my phone? I just had it!"

A motor had started, then faded. That had happened several times as people and police came and went. But this time was different. This time it was *her* motor. She looked behind them, where she'd skidded to a sloppy stop twenty yards away, outside the police tape. "Where the hell is my car?" she asked. And then she said, "Jack! Jack is taking my car!"

"You don't think he'd go after her alone, do you?" Dax asked.

"I wouldn't have thought it up 'til now, no."

Rob turned in a slow circle, one hand on his own head, like he was trying to force and idea into it. Then said, "We can track the watch from our computer back at the house. Come on, hurry."

Everyone piled into cars and took off for Holiday Ranch, pulling in about a minute later, spilling from their vehicles and swarming into the house. More relatives were arriving every second. Vidalia with her brood of daughters and all their husbands, and Sunny from the bakery, hanging close to Jason.

Kendra stood there waiting with the rest of them while Rob

tapped keys, and brought up a map. "That's out past the falls," he said. "Not even on a road."

"Tell me this ass hat is not making my pregnant sister hike through the woods," Kendra all but growled. They'd explored those woods as little girls, she recalled. It hadn't gone well.

"There's an old hunting cabin up near there," Rob said. "That's gotta be where they are."

"Then what are we waiting for?" Kendra looked at them expectantly.

Chief Jimmy held up a hand. "All right, listen. I know you all want to go up there, but you should leave this to the police. We need to be careful, we don't want to get her hurt."

Kendra looked at him, then looked around. "I don't know about the rest of you, but if you want to keep me here, you're gonna have to shoot me."

"I could arrest you," Jimmy said.

Rob clapped the chief on the shoulder. "No, Jim. You can't. She's family."

"Wouldn't be the first time," he replied with a look at Joey, meant to be teasing, and maybe break some of the tension. It failed. He sighed, and said, "We'll meet at the Brand family cabin, here." He touched a spot on the computer screen's map. "We'll have to hike in from there. And I don't want to see a single weapon on any of you."

"Don't worry." Kendra pressed her arm to her side, to cover the bulge in her pocket. "You won't."

∽

Kiley couldn't believe it when she heard someone knock on the shanty's wooden door.

She knew Rob would come for her. But she didn't expect him to knock.

Her captors didn't seem surprised though. "Mr. Caine"

looked up. Then he nodded at "Phil," who went to the door, lifted the 2 by 6 board that held it shut, and opened it.

Kiley's father walked in. She shot out of the rocking chair—shot being a relative term—and would've run into his arms, except that Caine pointed his ugly handgun at her and said, "Uh-uh-uh. Sit down."

Jack smiled, first at her face, and then at her belly. "You okay, Kiley-girl?"

"So far, so good, Dad," she said. "Does this all have something to do with you?"

"Yeah. And I'm sorry. I'm here to make it right."

Phil waved his gun. "Come on, Jack, you know the deal. Arms up."

Jack held his arms out to his sides, one a bit oddly, and as Phil patted him down, he said, "I missed you, too, you adorable ginger thug."

"He's clean, boss," Phil said.

"Where's Ace?" Jack looked from one man to the other. "Oh, he didn't have the stomach for kidnapping a pregnant woman, did he? Yeah, he's too decent for this kind of garbage. Well, no matter. Here I am, Caine. Alone and unarmed. Your demands have been met. You can let my daughter go now."

"Yeah, that's not exactly how this is gonna go down."

"I was afraid you'd say something like that." Then he shot Kiley a look, and she read it. He was going to do something. She was terrified, and opened her mouth to ask him not to, but too late. He grabbed Phil's shoulders and kneed him in the groin. Phil doubled over, and Jack shoved him so hard he stumbled backward and crached Caine. Caine's gun went off as his chair toppled. Jack clutched his thigh and collapsed to the floor. All of it had happened at the same time, and the next thing she knew, blood was pulsing from under her father's hand. Caine got up on his feet again.

Jack pushed himself up too and told her to run without a

word, his eyes shifting from her to the open door twice, filled with meaning. Then he lunged at Caine. Kiley raced out the door and into the woods. She had to get her baby to safety. And her father had just risked his life, maybe given his life, so that she could.

She would send someone back to save Jack. Maybe he'd still be okay.

Then something new happened that brought her dash through the forest to a sudden stop. It felt like a steel band was tightening around her middle. She clutched herself, fear, more than pain, just through her entire being.

Was that a contraction?

She couldn't rest. She had to keep moving. Caine would send his henchman after her. She had to get Diana to safety. So she clenched her jaw, and she ran.

∼

Dax had never seen Kendra's eyes look the way they did, perfectly round and kind of hollow. Like something had sucked all the life out of her.

They were hiking through the woods about a hundred yards out from the old hunting cabin where Kiley's watch was. Their goal was to circle behind the place and come in from the rear. They had the furthest distance to walk, but when they reached their goal spot, according to the GPS on his phone, no one else had yet checked in. Kendra brought the walkie-talkie up and pressed its button. "We're in place. Why aren't the rest of you?"

"Kendra, come on." Dax said it softly. He took the radio and said, "It's Dax and Kendra," he said. "We're ready."

"This is Rob, Joe and I are ready on the east side."

"Jason here. Sunny and I are ready on the west."

"Move in slow and quiet," Chief Corona said. "See if you can get a look inside," I'll assess. Do not do anything else until and unless I give the word."

"Hear that, Rob?" Dax asked, but his eyes were on Kendra.

Rob didn't reply, and Kendra didn't say a word either. She didn't have to. If she spotted her sister, she was going in, come hell or high water. He didn't know if he could stop her. He didn't know if he *should*.

He clipped the radio to his jeans. "I get why you've been deceiving me."

Kendra pushed a limb down to peer at the cabin. "I should've just told you the truth. That they had my father. Or that I *thought* they had my father." Shaking her head slowly, she said, "I can't believe he lied to me. I should've known. Kiley's right, I have a blind spot where he's concerned."

"It doesn't matter," Dax said. "I mean, as far as you and me."

"You and me? No, Dax. There is no you and me. Look at this, look at what I do to people. It's my fault all this came down on my sister. And sweet little Diana. And Rob. And you." She looked up at him, tears brimming in her eyes. Tears. He didn't think he'd ever seen her cry before. "You're good, Dax. I'm just…I'm bad. I'm bad, and, it's contagious. I can't wash it off like my sister did. It goes too deep in me. And it stains anything good that comes too close. I can't be with you, Dax. I'll *ruin* you. I'll ruin them, too."

"That's such a pile of horseshit." He reached for her, but she ducked away, turning from him and pressing the heel of her hand to her wet cheek.

"I've been kidding myself with this marketing thing, thinking I could live straight. Thinking I could change my own DNA."

"Kiley's your identical twin. Same DNA, right?"

"And yet my eyes are green, and hers are blue. We're opposites. Yin and Yang." She wiped a tear from her cheek like she was mad at it. "I've gotta go get my sister." Then she took off toward the back of the cabin like a ninja rabbit, staying low and darting from juniper to pinion pine. There were no tall grasses or brambles in between the trees. Just rich red earth, under a layer of decaying tree litter. Needles, leaves, twigs. Blossoms and berries, cones and bark. Every footfall released a waft of fragrance as he ran to catch up. He got a hand on her shoulder just as she reached the cabin's back wall, and pulled her into a crouch beside him underneath a window.

It wasn't a cabin so much as a shack. Its barn-board sides were so old the wood was bleached to Gandalf gray. The tin roof looked like it had been in a rusty rainstorm. There were two windows in the back, both made of thick plastic-glass. It had been there so long it was hazy.

"Easy now," Dax said. "You went too fast. The others aren't—"

She popped up, stopping with her eyes just above the bottom of the foggy plastic. "I can see a little. Jack's in there!" She dropped into a low crouch again, breathing fast. "He doesn't look good."

Dax rose just enough to see inside. A tall man in a suit paced back and forth in front of a rickety chair, smoking a cigar almost violently. Jack Kellogg was occupying said rickety chair. He looked like a duct tape mummy. His head was the only part of him not taped to the chair. His face was turning purple.

Dax looked around the inside of the cabin. One room. No partitions. There was a second man there, a big guy. He didn't see Kiley. Not unless she was hiding in a rear corner, beyond his line of sight.

Crouching low again, he took Kendra's hand and pulled her with him a few yards back, to the nearest tree. From behind it, he keyed the walkie-talkie. "I can see Jack Kellogg, duct taped to a chair and not looking too healthy. There are two other men, one I'm presuming to be Vester Caine. The other must be one of his goons. No sign of Kiley."

"Same here," came over the crackling radio.

"Same."

"Ditto."

"Where the hell is she?" That was Rob's voice. Dax didn't think he'd ever heard so much anguish in his life.

"Fuck this," Kendra said. "I'm done tiptoeing around these assholes." And like a shot, she was off and running toward the cabin. She didn't stop at the back this time, but darted around it toward the front.

Dax ran after her, radio in hand, "Kendra's going in! I can't stop her!" Then he jammed its clip onto his jeans and ran faster.

Kendra was at the front door. She slammed into it with her shoulder, and smashed right through. She had a gun in her hand when Dax burst in behind her. The two men stood there with their hands up, because Kendra was pointing her gun at them, more specifically, at the suit-wearing slick's head. "Twitch and you die," Kendra said.

There was a handgun on a nearby wooden table. Dax moved inside and picked it up.

"Cut Jack loose," Kendra shouted. "I think he's suffocating!"

Dax went to Jack. He wasn't conscious. His face had shifted from purple to blue-gray. They must've used the whole damn roll of duct tape wrapping him to the chair. Quickly, he took out a pocketknife and started slicing through all that tape. Others started to come in, but stopped in the doorway when they understood the situation.

Jimmy Corona crowded through and came up beside Kendra. "Put the gun down now. I've got this," he said.

"Where the hell is my sister, Caine?" He said nothing, so she moved the gun to the other guy, the redheaded muscle. "You. Talk. Where is Kiley?"

The thug didn't answer so she dropped the gun barrel low and shot him in the foot. Everybody jumped or yelled. Phil screamed and grabbed his foot, blood oozing through his shoe and around his hand.

"Try again," Kendra said. "Where is my sister?"

Chief Jimmy put a hand on her arm.

"You don't me, Chief, but believe me when I tell you that if you touch me again and I'll blow his head off."

He took his hand away.

"Where is my sister?"

"She got away," the bleeding thug said.

"Then why does her watch say she's still here?"

"Watch," he repeated it as if he'd only just then figured out something important.

Someone outside yelled, "Found her watch. She hid it in the outhouse."

"Clever little bitch," the bleeding thug said.

Kendra shot him in his other foot. The Chief Jimmy grabbed her arm and wrenched the weapon from her hands. Dax yanked her free of him and got in Jimmy's face. "That's enough!"

One of Jimmy's co-cops went to the thug who was writhing on the floor, while Dax held Kendra back. "I hope you never walk again, you worthless waste of oxygen."

Someone was on the radio, calling for help. Doc Sophie was doing CPR on Jack, who was on his back on the floor. His duct tape had been sliced down both sides and Darryl Champlain was peeling it off him while trying to stay out of his wife's way. There was a bandage wrapped tight around his thigh.

Kendra looked that way, and then she tipped her head back and howled at the ceiling in agony and rage.

Dax turned her toward him, hugged her to his chest, his big hands in her hair, stroking and cradling. "It's okay, it's okay. She got away."

"We've gotta find her," she cried against his chest. Then she picked her head up, and gazed up into his eyes. "It's getting dark. We've gotta *find* her!"

CHAPTER ELEVEN

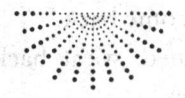

"If Kiley knew where she was, she'd have gone that way," Rob said, pointing toward the woods.

Kendra looked that way briefly, torn. She wanted to go to her father. Doc Sophie was still in the cabin working on him. He was dying. He was dead, maybe. If she was still pumping his chest, that meant he was dead, didn't it? Maybe he'd come back, but right now....

There was a Life-Flight chopper on its way to get him. Her heart was bleeding for Jack, but she had to save her sister. It's what he came here to do. He's be pissed if she didn't follow through. "Why do you think she'd go that way, Rob?"

"Edie and Wade's place is that way. It's not more than a mile if you cut through the woods at an angle."

"I don't think it was there when we were kids," Kendra said. "Does she know about it?"

"She does," Rob said. "We've been there."

"Fourth of July Brand-McIntyre family barbeque," Joey filled in.

"Then she might've gone that way. I don't know, though, she's always had the worst sense of direction. We need to split up. Cover more ground," she said. She looked around, trying to sense which direction Kiley would've taken. "I'm going this way." Kendra took off, stomping into the forest. Dax was on her heels.

Jimmy-police-chief Corona came to edge of the woods, calling after them. "Wait, wait, just give me two minutes so we can make sure we're not all covering the same ground! It'll save time later. Kendra, Dax, come back."

Kendra stopped, turned, went back to him, held out her hand. "I want my gun back."

"I can't—"

"Seriously, I don't want to end up like my old man."

"No."

"Kendra," Dax called.

She looked back at him. He tapped his backside. Holy shit, Dax was armed. He'd picked up the gun Phil had dropped.

She was rubbing off on him. That's wasn't a good thing, and she knew it, but at this moment, she was glad. She headed into the woods. They were familiar. She'd been there before.

They were nine years old. She and Kiley had sneaked away from a nice cabin, farther down the hillside, where they'd been having a camping weekend with their Dad. He said he had permission from the owners, but Kendra knew better. He'd had to pick the lock to get them in. You didn't pick locks when you had permission. But she understood her dad's point of view, too. Perfectly good cabin sitting there empty most of the year. Rich people didn't have any sense.

At four a.m., barely daylight, she and Kiley had sneaked out to go on an adventure.

"What time you think it is now?" Kiley had asked. She was peering through the trees with her elbow over her eyes trying to see the sun, but she was looking too high up.

"It's gotta be seven. Dad'll be awake by eight," Kendra told her.

Kiley dropped her arm and looked at her with wide eyes. "That's not enough time to get back!"

"So what?" Kendra started back down the deer trail they'd followed.

"We'll get in trouble," Kiley said. "I *hate* getting in trouble."

"It's not a big deal. What's he gonna do? Ground us to our rooms when we get home? Who cares? We got TVs in our rooms."

"We're going on that field trip to the Astrobleme Museum Friday."

"Riiiight," Kendra said, slowing down so Kiley could walk alongside her. "This is gonna get us out of that, for sure."

"But I *wanna* go!"

"Why?"

Kiley shrugged. "Because I've never seen it before. A meteor crater eight miles wide? Come on. How can you not want to see that? I love seeing things I've never seen before." Then she hung her head. "But now I won't get to see it. Maybe I'll never see it."

Kendra sighed and looked around. "Maybe there's a shortcut. That road was really twisty." Then she heard the soft sounds of bubbling, tumbling water. "Streams run downhill, and streams feed the waterfall. Our cabin—"

"It's not our cabin."

"It is today. Our cabin is within sight of the waterfall. So we follow the stream downhill." And off she went, feeling pretty damn good about herself because for once, she'd been smarter than Kiley. Yes, Kendra was the leader, and also the best at Jack's lessons, but Kiley was the smart one. Most of the time.

Turned out later she hadn't been so smart after all. They'd spotted the cabin and taken off running, and it had turned into a race, and they were so damn competitive. Kendra more so than Kiley. But this time Kiley pulled ahead of her, and then she ran right off a....

Kiley ran right off a cliff.

She'd dashed out the door of the shack, and left her poor father behind, not knowing if he would die because of it. She'd had no choice. She'd taken off at a dead run—which in her shape, was more like a headlong wobble. As she went deeper into the woods, she was mentally calculating the fastest route to Edie and Wade's gorgeous A-frame and angling in the direction she thought it would be.

She hadn't gone very far when the tightening sensation came again. It hurt, and she didn't think it should, not this soon. Labor took a long time. Especially for first-timers. Every female in Big Falls who'd managed to reproduce, and most of those of those who hadn't, had told her so.

She pressed her back to a tree until the pressure eased, and while she waited, she listened. But she didn't hear anyone giving chase. Not yet. Maybe Caine didn't care. God, she hoped her father was okay. That was damn heroic, what he did back there. He had to have known the risk.

Who knew he had it in him?

She had to get to a house, to a phone, to Rob. She had to find a safe place to have her baby, and send help back for her dad. She wished she'd told him. She should have told him. He was going to be a grandfather. He wasn't all bad. He might've given his life for her baby's back there.

She loved him.

As soon as the contraction eased, she took off again, as fast as she could, and then she stopped again to let the pain pass, and then she ran again. This went on right up until a twig snapped while she was moving, which made her run even faster while looking back over her shoulder in terror.

And then suddenly, there was nothing under her feet, and she was falling. She hit the sloping side, scraping and banging over dirt and stone and continuing to plummet. She kept her arms around her belly as best she could, and prayed for it to end.

When she finally came to a stop, every part of her screamed in pain. And she laid there, panting, hurting, terrified.

She pushed herself up a little, just enough to see her baby bump and run her hands over it. "Move," she whispered. "Move, Diana. Show Mamma you're okay."

Another contraction came. It was so powerful she yelped. But Diana hadn't kicked.

She tried to breathe through it until it ebbed. She ought to be timing them, but she'd left her damn watch... *oh, God, why didn't I grab the watch from the outhouse when I left? They could've found me. God only knows where I am.*

She licked her lips and looked around her, praying for something familiar.

And it floated back to her. This whole *thing* was familiar. God, why didn't she remember sooner? How could she go running off the edge of the world in the same exact spot twice?

Another contraction came. "No. It's too soon. They're too close." She held on for dear life and blew puffs of air through her lips.

~

Kendra stopped in her tracks as she heard her sister scream.

Dax charged past her, running like the hero he was. "Dax don't! There's a—" Too late. He'd vanished. She heard him grunting as he tumbled. "Drop-off," she finished, lamely.

She ran to the edge, then skirted it until she found a slightly less vertical slope, and scrambled down, sliding, falling, catching herself, and eventually reaching the bottom. Dax was right where he'd landed, his leg bent at an impossible angle underneath him. Kiley lay not far from him, her back against a tree, her face wet with tears, her breaths coming too fast.

"You okay, Dax?" she asked as she ran to her sister and fell to her knees beside her.

He said, "Yeah. Kiley?"

Kendra brushed her sister's hair off her face. "I'm here, Kiley. I'm here. Everything's okay now."

"I'm in labor," Kiley whispered. Kendra thought her heart stopped. "Is Dax okay?"

"I'm all right," Dax said. He was making his way to them, dragging himself along the forest floor. Kendra could see the strain on his face. He was hurting. "I lost the damn radio on the way down. Still got the gun, though."

"Gun?" Kiley asked, wide-eyed, terrified.

"I've got my cell." Kendra yanked it out, held it up. No bars. "Dammit." She scanned the slope for the walkie-talkie, but then Kiley cried out again.

"I want Rob!" There were tears in her voice. "The baby's coming, Kendra. She's coming!"

Kendra looked at Dax, who'd braced himself up against an adjacent sapling. "Dax, what are we gonna do?"

"We're gonna help your sister have a baby," he told her. And he said it so calmly she almost believed him. He took off his coat, wincing every time he moved. She looked at his leg. It was bent in a way shin bones should not bend. Her stomach lurched. "Hey," he said. Then he tossed her "Turn it inside out and lay that underneath her. "Then go wash your hands in the stream. I wish we had some damn soap."

Kendra hurried to obey, helping Kily lift her hips up and sliding the coat underneath. Then she ran to the stream, nearby and thrust her hand into the icy cold water. It felt good. She heard Dax talking softly to her sister, easing Kiley's panic as she hurried back. She tried to quell her own fear, or at least keep it hidden. She took off her own jacket, covered her sister with it.

Kiley started moaning and breathing too fast.

"Hey, hey, Kiley," Dax said. "Look at me, look me right in the eye." She turned to face him. "We've got this. You know how many foals I've helped into the world? We've got this, hon. You're gonna be okay. So's Diana."

"What if she was hurt in the fall?"

"She was riding along in a liquid-filled beach ball. She's fine. Say it now. Diana is fine."

"Diana's fine." She took a few fast breaths, nodding. "She's fine."

"We need to get you undressed okay? Kendra, can you help with that?"

Kendra looked at him, saw him in a way she'd never seen him before. But she snapped out of it and slid Kiley's pants off. Kiley bent her knees and pressed them to the ground, and blew rapid, short breaths.

"God, Dax, you really think we can do this?"

"Kiley's doin' this. We're just helping. I know a fair bit about birthing. Now tell me what you see, I can't get over there very well just now."

"I see... something," Kendra said. "Is that her *head*?"

"I need to push!"

Dax said, "Kendra, you need to check the cord..."

"I need to *push*!" This was happening way faster than Kendra had expected. The baby's head was already coming out.

"She's...purple," Kendra said.

Dax sat up straight. "Stop pushing. Blow, Kiley, blow little puffs. Don't push. Kendra, you have to use your fingers to make sure the cord isn't around the baby's neck. Do it now."

Kendra ran her fingers around the neck, found the cord wrapped tight there. "Hold back, don't push, I mean it Kiley!" she told her sister.

Kiley panted, blew, whimpered. Kendra knelt there, freaking out, working to loosen the cord from around the baby's neck without tearing it, which she sensed would be bad. It took some doing, but she got it loose. "Okay, Kiley, it's okay now."

Kiley growled and pushed, and the baby's head emerged, followed quickly by her shoulders, and then the rest of her. Kendra caught her, and Dax tossed his shirt at her. Diana wasn't moving. She wasn't moving! Kendra looked at Dax, then at the baby again as she wrapped her in the shirt.

"What is it?" Kiley tried to sit up to see. "What's wrong?"

"Turn her sideways," Dax said. "Clear her airways. Give her good rubdown.

Kendra did everything he said. "Come on, Diana. Come on, now."

"She's not breathing? Why isn't she breathing?" Kiley pushed herself upright and stared at her child. "Oh no!" She clapped a hand over her mouth.

Kendra didn't think she'd ever willed anything the way she willed that baby to live. Impulsively, she leaned over, covered the baby's nose and mouth with her own and gave three tiny puffs.

As she lifted her head away, the baby wiggled. And then she wailed. It was a congested, snuffly sound as was every newborn's first cry.

Smiling so hard her face hurt, her tears flowing, Kendra gazed at the scrunched, rapidly pinkening face. "Hello, Diana. I'm your aunt Kendra. And this is your mamma." She eased the baby into Kiley's arms, "She's okay. She's okay, Kiley."

She watched Kiley gather the baby to her, saw the bliss in her sister's eyes, and the way Diana's seemed to stare right into them, like she knew her. Shaking her head, she turned to Dax, and saw a big old tear roll slowly down over his cheek.

She crawled to him, wrapped her arms around his neck and held on.

Voices came from the rim of the drop-off. Kendra looked up sharply. "Is that the rest of the gang?"

But then the sound crackled oddly, and Dax said, "That's the walkie-talkie. I must've dropped it on the way down." The sound was coming from the top of the ridge.

"Perfect timing. Stay here. Take care of them. I'll climb up and get that radio, guide the others in."

Kiley sniffled. "Kendra?"

Kendra went to her. "You did great. Rob's gonna be so proud."

"You saved us," she whispered. "Just like always. I love you so much, Kendra." She locked an arm around Kendra's neck and hugged her hard.

"I love you, too." She gazed down at the baby. Diana had stopped crying. She had an elfin face, a face like a newborn fairy child, and wide eyes of the darkest, wettest blue-black-slate she'd ever seen. They were magic, those eyes.

"I'm gonna go get help, okay? Your doting husband is worried sick."

"Okay. Don't go far, Kendra. I need you."

"Yeah," Dax said. "Don't go far. I need you, too."

∽

Kendra was in awe of Dax Russell, the guy she thought she knew already. She hadn't had a clue, though. She'd thought he was soft, but he was strong. She'd thought he was sweet, but he was good. He was just *good*. Too good for the likes of her.

She found a spot to climb up the hill. It was cold, and she'd given her jacket to her sister. Dax was down there shirtless. At least she was moving. The effort warmed her a little. She got to the top of the drop off, and then looked back and waved at the three people she loved most in the whole world. Then she moved along the ridge at the top, back to the spot where Dax had fallen over. Sure enough, the radio was there in the dirt near the edge. She picked it up and keyed the mic. "I found her.

Everything's fine. There's a steep drop. She and Dax are at the bottom."

"Kendra, be careful!" She didn't recognize the voice. Was it Chief Jimmy? "Caine got away."

"What?"

"He said, 'Caine got away,'" Vester Caine said. He was standing behind her. She turned around slowly. She glanced at the radio.

"Not another word. Put the radio down."

Her thumb was working the transmit button, depressing it and releasing it, 3 times quickly, 3 times slowly 3 times quickly. She got two S.O.S. sequences out before dropping the radio to ground, and then "accidentally" kicking it over the side.

"Come with me."

"What the hell do you want, Caine? You got Jack. You had your revenge. Didn't you see how bad off he was back there?"

"He's still alive. Or was. They choppered him out of there after you left. I should've killed him right away, but I thought I might need a hostage to get out of there. They took Phil by chopper, too. You should've shot me instead of him. Why didn't you?"

"I knew he'd talk if I hurt him. You wouldn't have."

He pressed his lips and nodded slowly. "You're right, I wouldn't." He waved the gun barrel. "This way. Move."

She didn't look back. Maybe he didn't realize Jack's other daughter, and grandchild were so nearby. She moved quickly, to put distance between them before the baby cried or one of them called her name. But the path he made her take led around the top of the ridge, so they were circling, rather than moving away from them. Dax would take care of Kiley and the baby until help arrived. And if help didn't arrive, he'd carry them both down off this hill on his back, one-legged. She didn't doubt it a bit. All she had to do was keep this animal from noticing them down there.

"So you're gonna kill me to get back at Jack for stealing your whiskey and cigars? Is that what this is?"

"I oughtta kill you for what you did to Phil. You know how hard it is to get good help these days?"

"Right. I bet soulless thugs are hard to come by."

"They are. But no. I'm not gonna kill you. Not yet anyway. I need to get across the border."

"Mexico?" He didn't answer, but she was sure he had a billion-dollar spread south of the border. Heroin was big business. All this wasn't even going to put a wrinkle in his silk sheets.

"Follow that trail there," he said, wagging the gun.

The trail he indicated circled around drop-off, and the place at the bottom where Kiley had given birth. It kept them too close. She wanted to get him to move further away from them.

"Why this way? I think the road is over here. If we cut through—"

"The road is the way we're going," he said. She didn't know if he was right or wrong, didn't know how he thought he knew, and didn't care. "Move it."

She sighed, and kept walking. Maybe if she just went fast enough, they could get around the other side, and out of earshot before the baby cut loose another wail.

～

Dax heard Kendra's voice on the radio, and then heard the radio tumbling and banging its way down the face of the drop-off. It followed the path he'd taken down himself.

"What was that?" Kiley asked.

He held up a hand so she'd go quiet, just in case, and scanned the ground until he spotted the walkie-talkie lying at the bottom. Then he looked up in time to see two forms moving off into the trees.

Two forms.

"Something's wrong, isn't it?"

He glanced at Kiley. "Keep the baby as quiet as you can, okay?" Then he crawled on two hands and one knee, dragging the broken leg behind him. Pain screamed all the way to his teeth, but he kept it contained, grabbed the walkie. "Anyone there?" He spoke as softly as he could, and turned the volume down while awaiting a response.

Rob's voice came back. "We're on our way. Be careful, Caine got away from Jimmy. Cracked him over the head with a rock and ran off through the woods. I was just telling Kendra that when she started keying in an SOS, then went silent. What happened?"

He glanced upward again, then a twig snapped further away, drawing his gaze. He turned the radio off, scanning the trees to the right of them. And he saw them, shadows in the trees, Kendra in front, and a man behind her.

Caine.

He slid a look Kiley's way. The look on her face told him she'd seen it, too. He nodded at her, gave a stay calm gesture with his palm. Then he got his leg out in front of him, gripped his shin with both hands, and yanked the broken bone back into place. The sound was sickening, the pain more so. Kiley clapped a hand over her mouth. He sat there, hands on the break. He didn't have time to wait long, though. He looked around, located a long, sturdy looking limb, and slid closer. Then he got up on one leg and, using the limb as a crutch, hobbled across the little clearing.

Kendra and Caine seemed to be circling it, making their way to the lower side by going around rather than over the drop. The road must be in that direction.

He kept the gun in his jeans, its metal cold against his bare back, and moved as quickly and quietly as he could to the bottom edge of their clearing. Then he pulled the gun out, looked at it, and shaking his head, put it back. He couldn't shoot a man.

They were coming closer. He positioned himself near the edge of the animal trail they seemed to be following, behind a crooked pine tree, stood on one leg, and picked up his crutch.

They came into sight. He waited. They moved closer. They stepped right in front of his spot. The baby started to cry. Cain and his gun swung in that direction. Kendra turned and grabbed his gun hand, getting right between it and the baby, so its barrel was aimed at her chest as she yanked on his arm. Dax hopped out and brought the crutch down like a sledge hammer on Caine's head.

The limb broke right in half. Dax pulled out the damn gun as Cain spun around, yanking Kendra right off her feet, but she did not let go of that arm.

"Drop it or I'll yank your arm out of its socket you dirty rotten—" She sank her teeth into his forearm. He punched her in the face with his free hand and she dropped to the ground like a sack of feed.

Dax shot him. The bullet hit him in the right shoulder, spinning him right around, and Kendra jumped up onto her feet, snatched Caine's gun from him easily, and backed up until she was standing beside Dax. Cain dropped to his knees, clutching his bleeding shoulder. "I hate you fucking Kelloggs."

"Should'a aimed for his head," Kendra said. She glanced sideways at him, saw the pain on his face. He wobbled, and she wrapped her arm around his waist. "Lean on me, big guy."

He put an arm around her. There were people running, crashing through the woods by then. Chief Jimmy Corona, a nasty wound on his head all swollen and cut. It had bled all over his face. He walked up behind Caine and handcuffed him, in spite of the shoulder wound. Caine yelped in pain but no one cared.

Rob shouted for Kiley, and she called back. He ran to her,

wrapped her and the baby in his arms and held them. Dax couldn't see his face, but he'd bet there were tears on it.

Four wheelers growled from a distance, the BFFD had come to the rescue.

Dax squeezed Kendra's shoulders. "Long day, huh?"

She let her head fall onto his shoulder, watching her sister's little family embracing a few yards away. "Long day," she agreed. "You did so good, Dax."

"So did you, Kendra. You *are* good. You just don't know it, is all."

CHAPTER TWELVE

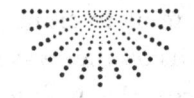

THANKSGIVING DAY

Kendra stood in the Long Branch, feeling out of place, and knowing more than before that the decision she'd made was the right one.

The place was hopping with Brands and McIntyres, all of them happy and smiling and beautiful and good. People were carrying piping hot dishes from the kitchen to the long tables set up in the dining room. There were immaculate linen tablecloths all patterned in russet leaves and cornucopias. There were centerpieces of sunflowers, yellow mums and burgundy carnations. The place settings were perfect, with colorful cloth napkins in mustard yellow. The area near the front windows had been cleared of tables. Tomorrow, Kiley told her, they'd put up a Christmas tree there.

Dax hadn't arrived yet. Kendra was nervous about seeing him again. She had barely exchanged three sentences with him in the days since Diana's birth in the woods. She'd been busy with her father in the hospital, with her sister and new niece. He'd been busy, too, making a deal with the New York State attorney general. His mother wasn't going to be prosecuted. In exchange, she and Dax were cooperating fully with the state in its prosecution of Vester Caine. They'd turned over the books, and the track's bookkeeper had been arrested. Vester was in custody, and Phil was in a hospital, but handcuffed to the bed. Chief Jimmy swore Kendra had fired her weapon in self-defense. No one questioned it.

Ace was still at large.

Kiley said Dax was coming to dinner, but Kendra was a little afraid that he wouldn't. His mother was there, though, with Luis Mendosa. They seemed completely in love. Miss Dolly and Ned could barely keep their hands off each other. Everyone was mingling, nibbling appetizers and the piano was playing them a selection of old timey holiday music.

When Vidalia came out of the kitchen with a picture perfect roasted turkey on a platter, and her husband Bobby Joe came out behind her with another, the oohs, ahhs and praise were universal. And then they were all gathering around the giant tables.

"Oh, we can't begin yet," Miss Dolly said. "Not everyone is here."

"They are now."

It was Dax!

Kendra couldn't help the relief that rushed through her at the sound of his voice, or the shiver of awareness up her spine. She turned toward the batwing doors way past the open red velvet curtains, and then blinked in surprise. Dax was pushing a wheelchair, and her father was its passenger. They were both dressed in suits and ties and they were both smiling.

"Jack?" Kendra asked.

"Dad!" Kiley shouted, and they both went to the doorway to greet him.

"Hello girls." Jack flashed his dimples around the room. "Thank you for the invitation Miz Vidalia."

Dax had hold of Kendra's eyes and wouldn't let go. The conversation, the greetings, were happening all around them. But they were apart from all of it.

"You're family, Jack," Vidalia said. "You don't need an invitation, but I wasn't sure you knew that yet."

Jack spotted Rob holding the baby while Kiley was hugging his neck and asking how he got out a day sooner than planned. He didn't really answer. Instead he said, "If it's okay with everyone, I'd really like to have a word with my granddaughter."

"And I'd like to have word with you, Kendra," Dax said. His voice was all hoarse. "Outside, if that's okay?"

She looked at him frowned. "Actually, I need to talk to you too."

She grabbed her jacket from a hook, and he opened the door for her. They stepped out into the parking lot, him hobbling on one crutch. He said, "Your sister tells me you're leaving tomorrow."

"I wasn't going without saying goodbye to you first," she said. "I just...it's been...."

"I know."

"I was gonna pick Jack up on the way, take him with me. Didn't expect this."

"He's not going," Dax said.

Kendra blinked, stunned. "What, now? What do you mean, he's not going?"

"We had a long talk, your dad and me. He said he saw your mother, during that time when his heart wasn't beating. Said she told him to get his ass back here and be a good grandfather to her namesake."

She frowned. "He didn't...tell me any of that."

"He will. When he's ready. He's still...processing it, I think. Point is, he says he's going straight. Moving back here to Big Falls to be with his family."

She turned in a slow circle, tipped her head back, closed her eyes. "He can't do that."

"He can if he wants. It's a free country. And I don't know how you're can leave Kiley to ride herd on him all by herself. Do you?" He touched her shoulders, turned her to face him again. He was looking at her like he was trying to memorize her face.

"I'll make him see sense," she said. "We can come and visit."

"Well, you know, that's between you and your father, I guess."

She nodded, and decided the moment had come. She pulled her keys out of her jacket pocket and held them out.

"What's this?" he asked.

"I'm paying you back," she said. "The 'Vette's worth way more than half of what I took you for. Maybe three quarters. But I'm gonna pay back the rest, too."

He nodded, took the keys from her. "That's way more than enough."

She nodded. She'd expected him to argue harder. But it didn't matter. She'd intended make him take it, even if he did.

"I'm staying in Big Falls too." He put her keys in his pocket, fiddled around in there for a second. "There's a place for sale five miles west of town that's exactly what I want. I'm buying it. Gonna put in a track, train horses there."

She nodded slowly. "That's great, Dax. I can really see that for you."

"Can you see it for you?"

She lowered her head, unable to hold his eyes. "I can't. Dax, I'm not good enough for this town, or that baby in there, or even my own sister anymore. And I'm nowhere near good enough for you."

"I've said that about myself a million times. That I'm not good enough for you." He took a deep breath. "But here's the thing. I know you, Kendra Kellogg. I know you better than you know yourself. I saw your face out there, delivering little Diana. It was the face of an angel."

"An angel who almost got my whole family killed."

"You didn't do that. Jack did that, and let me tell you, he regrets it to his bones. Something profound happened to your father in that cabin, Kendra. It changed him. I think all of this has changed you, too. And I think you know it, deep down, and you're just too scared to trust that it's for real. That it will last."

She nodded, recognizing truth when she heard it. "You're right. You're right, I *am* afraid of that. And afraid of what it would do to you, and to my poor sister, if I tried and failed. And what about Diana? What if I make her love me, make her trust me, and then I fail miserably? What if—"

"And what if you don't? What if you succeed? What if you would've succeeded, but you're too scared to even try? Wouldn't that be the real tragedy?"

She lowered her head. "I don't know. I don't know how to be sure of anything."

"No one is ever sure what's going to happen in the future, Kendra. You can only be sure of the present. This one moment. All you can be is here, now. Any one of us could be gone tomorrow. If this whole experience taught us anything, it should be that. We have to make the most of every single day of our lives. Don't you believe that?"

She frowned. "I...I do. I do believe that."

"That's a start. Now let's try one more. Which is more important? Love or fear?"

"L-love?"

"Yeah, love. You love your sister. You love Diana. You even love that rascal, Jack. How can you just walk away from all that love by choosing fear instead?"

Kendra lowered her head. She paced a few steps away from him, and then a few steps back.

"You love *me*, Kendra. I know you do. I can see it in your eyes, and I can feel it every time you touch me. You love me. You love me as much as I love you, and that's a helluva lot."

He hobbled closer, touched her chin, tipped it up. "Deny it. I dare you."

And then before she could say anything, he kissed her. He kissed her long and slow and so tenderly that tears leaked from her eyes, slid down her cheeks and salted their lips. He lifted his head and said, "I love you, Kendra Kellogg."

"I...love you too," she admitted.

"I'm not gonna let you fail."

She smiled through tears. "What, you have super powers or something?"

"I have magic," he said. "Wanna see?"

Sniffling, she nodded. "Sure."

He looked up at the sky. "Which one's your favorite star?" She just frowned at him and he said, "Just pick one. You want to see magic or not?"

She knuckled her wet cheek, and pointed at the brightest star in sight.

"Good choice." Dax reached up, stretching his long arm out. He mimicked plucking the star from the sky, lowered his fisted hand, and then opened it, palm up. A diamond ring rested there.

Awkwardly, and painfully, he dropped to one knee while she was still blinking in shock.

"There's no other woman for me, Kendra. You're all I want, all I've ever wanted. I love you. I want us to build a life together right here in Big Falls. I want spend the rest of my life showing you how good you really are. And I'd kind of like to be Diana's official uncle."

She looked down at him for a long moment.

"Get out of your head, woman. Just be in the moment. What do you want to do, right now?"

"I want to say yes," she said.

"Then say it."

Her lips pulled into a smile. "Yes. I'll marry you." She helped him upright and he slid that ring onto her finger, swept her into his arms and kissed her, bending her backward over his arm.

A cheer went up from nearby, and they jumped apart, startled.

Dozens of happy faces were peering out through the big front windows. The window opened. Vidalia leaned out and said, "Congratulations, you two. Now, can we *please* eat before my perfect turkey dries up and blows away?"

∽

As they sat among their family, passing dishes around the table, Vidalia said, "I'll go first," and she winked at Kendra. "Family tradition. Ahem. I am thankful for this family, and how it keeps growing and expanding and bringing joy and love into my life."

Ned spoke up next. He was sitting next to Miss Dolly, and he gazed right into her eyes and said, "I'm thankful for the most charming lady I've ever met, and that she has family here in Big Falls now, giving her an excuse to stick around."

Dolly winked at him. "I didn't need any excuse, once I set eyes on you, Ned."

Rob said, "I'm thankful for my two girls, Kiley and Diana. I don't think any man's ever been so blessed."

"I have," Joey said. "I've got two fine girls myself to be thankful for."

"I'm thankful for my new cousin!" Matilda Louise sang. "I'm gonna teach her everything! How to braid hair, how to paint her toenails, how to ride a pony!"

"You don't know how to ride a pony," Emily told her daughter.

"First, I'll learn, then I'll teach Diana." She turned to her father very seriously. "So I'm *really* gonna need a pony for Christmas *this* year."

Everyone laughed.

Caroline said, "I'm grateful that there's a wedding to plan!" Then gazing at Luis, "And that I have someone I love to dance with at the reception."

Jack cleared his throat, and everyone looked his way. He'd aged, Kendra thought. He was pale, seemed frail sitting in that wheelchair. But his blue eyes were still just as sparkling, and his dimples, just as deep.

"I'm thankful for a second chance," he said. "I'm thankful that my girls led me back here. This is a special town. My wife always said so. I'm gonna be a better grandfather than I was a father." He shrugged. "That's not saying much, I guess. I was a pretty bad father. But I'm gonna really try to do this grandpa thing up right. And I'm thankful to have two strong, smart daughters who'll kick me in the nu—" Everyone gasped. "Knuckles," he went on. "If I mess up."

Kendra nodded. For the first time, she believed Jack was serious. She took a breath, and took her turn. "I'm thankful for more than I can even list. For all of you in this room, and how you welcomed me back here when you knew what I'd been. For my sister and my precious niece. For my dad, surviving what should've done him in. And for Dax Russell, a guy who believes in me more than I believe in myself." She looked Dax right in the eye. "You make me want to live up to that belief. And sitting here with all of you, I'm starting to think I can."

Dax raised his glass. "Happy Thanksgiving," he said. And then he slipped her car keys, into her lap under the table and leaned close to whisper, "Engagement present."

Everyone held up their glasses, even the children, and chorused, "Happy Thanksgiving!"

Kendra touched her glass to Dax's and gazed into his eyes. "The happiest ever," she said softly.

"Only so far," he replied.

–The End–

**Continue reading for an excerpt from book 5
in the McIntyre Men series
Baby By Christmas.**

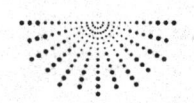

PREVIEW BABY BY CHRISTMAS

CHAPTER ONE

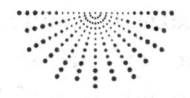

MARCH 29TH

Alexis Wakeland had never started a bar fight before. It would probably surprise her family to hear that. She'd always been the black sheep, the one the others rolled their eyes at when they thought she wasn't looking. She was the hellion who got into more trouble than the rest of her siblings put together, the one who made bad choices and couldn't admit she was wrong. Despite all that, she'd never once been the cause of a barroom brawl––until tonight.

All she'd wanted was a fun night out with her big brother. A couple of drinks and laughs before he deployed to Afghanistan. You couldn't blame her for being sentimental. She was afraid she'd never see him again.

Like Jeff. Angie's husband had died over there. And now Allie's big sister was a widow, raising two kids alone.

Poor little Jack still refused to believe his daddy was really gone.

Allie would never *ever* be a military wife. It couldn't possibly be worth that kind of pain. Some days she couldn't imagine how her big sister managed to get out of bed every morning, and face every day without Jeff. The two had always been like clouds and sky, inseparable. One couldn't exist without the other.

Yet somehow, her sister kept going.

And their brother Adam was deploying tomorrow.

Adam was also talking to her, but she wasn't listening. "I love you, you know," she blurted.

He was quiet for a second. Then he said, "I love you, too. And I'm coming home, Lexie. I promise."

His pet name for her made her eyes get wet. No one else called her Lexie. "You friggin' better." She pressed the heel of her hand to her cheek to absorb a rogue tear and, for once, didn't hate him for it.

"I'm sorry I can't make it tonight."

She tapped the phone's volume button. Adam's voice was hard to make out in the noisy bar. "You didn't just say what I think you said, did you? I'm already here."

"It's an emergency. I wouldn't stand you up if there was any way to get out of it."

Allie rolled her eyes. Everything to do with his job was always an emergency with her brother. He ought to have the word "duty" tattooed on his forehead. And whatever the issues, he was always sure he was the only person who could possibly handle it.

"Does this mean I won't get to see you before you go?" she asked, trying to mask the disappointment in her voice. It was hard though, because her throat went tight in the middle of the question.

"Of course not. Let's get up early and have breakfast tomorrow morning."

She was still disappointed, but she knew she had to swallow her emotions. She wasn't going to send him off on the memory of her being a petulant brat. It would just confirm his belief that she was still thirteen. "I'll take what I can get," she told him.

"Good," he said. "And when I say early, I mean early. Don't stay out partying all night."

Allie sighed. She shouldn't be surprised by his assumption. She shouldn't be hurt by it, either. The truth was she rarely drank anymore. Not since college, but her family had built an image of her as the crazy party girl, and arguing wouldn't change that. Angie said the only thing that would ever change it was time. The self-help book on her night stand said the only thing that could ever change it was *her*.

"Allie?"

"I'd have called it a night already if I hadn't been waiting for you." That probably sounded defensive. "I'll see you in the morning, big brother. Early."

"Night, kid," he said.

Allie tapped the end button on her phone and dropped it into her bag with a sigh. This was not how she'd pictured the evening going, but as long as she got to see her brother before he left, she'd be content.

She drained the last of her drink--rum and diet with a splash of grenadine--and decided to head back to her hotel room. Fort Sill, Oklahoma wasn't so far from home that she couldn't have made the trip back to Big Falls, but she'd vowed to do the responsible thing, and plan ahead, just in case she had a couple drinks with her brother. She wasn't about to get behind the wheel after she'd had a drink, not that her family would believe that.

What other people think of me is none of my business, she reminded herself.

Mentally reciting quotes from self-help books usually calmed her, but not when it came to her family.

She pushed herself to her feet, wobbling a little on the heels of her boots. Stupid choice in footwear, she thought. Sneakers were her usual choice, but she'd wanted to dress up for a night on the town. It had been so long since she'd had one, she'd let herself get a little excited about it. She glanced down at the skinny black jeans that hugged her legs all the way to her knee-high boots and smiled a little.

Uncomfortable, but worth it. She looked damn good.

Allie took another step, trying hard not to wobble. The rum was hitting her harder than she'd realized. She'd skipped lunch, and she couldn't remember the last time she'd had a drink. Ever since her brother in law Jeff had been killed in action, she'd been on high alert, ready to run to Angie's house any time she was needed. And she'd been needed a lot. *Thank God for our family*, she thought. And then she smiled, because she'd just been complaining about them in her head a moment ago.

Another careful step. She looked up to make sure she wasn't about to run into anyone, but as soon as her gaze left the floor, the heel of her boot caught on something. She tried to regain her balance. Her arms flailed in front of her, but it was no use. She stumbled forward and slammed into a hard chest.

A strong arm wrapped around her waist to steady her. She looked up into warm blue eyes and a face so handsome she couldn't catch her breath for a second. Everything froze, and then switched to ultra-slow motion. The handsome stranger's glass flew right over his head and crashed into the big, angry looking guy behind him. The angry guy lunged toward him, and Handsome shoved her backward out of his path. She stumbled, tripped over her heels and fell to the floor, bumping her head on a table on the way down.

"Hey!" She was too surprised to utter anything more intelligent. But it didn't matter, because the word was barely out of her mouth before the good-looking stranger crashed onto the floor, too.

His head landed on her chest and she felt a mix of embarrassment and excitement. She knew she should move, stand up, get out of there. Something. But all she could do was gape at the man lying on top of her.

His eye was red and puffy.

That big guy hit him.

It seemed her brain was functioning again at last. Allie glanced toward the bar and saw the meaty giant, beer still dripping down his face. He was advancing fast.

The man on her lap shot her a killer smile, apparently unconcerned with the brute. The puffy eye should have messed up his good looks instead of adding a rugged and irresistible appeal. When he grinned, a dimple appeared in his cheek, and a chill tap-danced up her spine.

"There are easier ways to get a man's attention," he said.

"Believe it or not, I wasn't throwing myself at your feet."

"No? Maybe I'm throwing myself at yours, then."

"Cute, but how about you get off me before you have two shiners instead of just one?"

His grin widened. Not exactly the desired effect, but she had to admit that smile was almost enough to make her forget to be annoyed with the guy.

He pushed himself to his feet and held out a hand to her. She grabbed it grudgingly and started to pull herself up when he suddenly let go again. She plunked right back onto the floor.

"Even less funny the second time," she muttered.

The big guy at the bar had finally made his way through the crowd. He was holding the front of her new friend's shirt and was about to punch him again, but a dazzling smile and brilliant blue eyes weren't her rescuer's only strengths. He dodged the blow, twisted free, grabbed her by the hand and pulled her with him toward the exit.

"I hope you're worth all this trouble," he said.

She wanted to tell him he'd never find out, but the hulk was already in pursuit, shoving people aside or plowing over them.

They pushed out through the door, into the cool March wind. It had been much warmer when she'd walked into the bar earlier. But the sun had set, and now it was raining. The temperature had dropped by at least ten degrees, and the wind made it feel even colder. Allie glanced behind them, but didn't see any sign they were being followed.

She was still a little shocked at the direction the night had taken. And he was still holding her hand.

"Sorry about your drink...and your face." She pulled her hand out of his. Her palm tingled where he'd held it. The danger seemed to be behind them, but adrenaline was still pumping through her system and she felt warm and tingly, despite the weather.

"I'm Logan," he said. "And you are?"

"Leaving." She said it fast, before she could talk herself out of it.

"That's cold. I just got decked because of you, and you're not even gonna tell me your name?"

"I'm Allie," she answered before she realized she was going to.

"Beautiful name. It suits you."

Allie rolled her eyes. "Does that line usually work?"

"Give me a break, I just got my face smashed in by Lou Ferrigno. My material is bound to be a little off."

"Only a little? Did Ferrigno scramble your brains, or are you just really bad at pick-up lines?"

Logan's eyes sparkled with mischief. "I have other assets."

That much was perfectly clear, she thought, trying to resist the urge to glance at the muscles she had felt so clearly before, when he'd been lying on top of her on the barroom floor. His t-shirt and leather jacket did nothing to hide the hard planes of his chest, and those sinfully tight jeans made her think all kinds of things she shouldn't be thinking. She forced her eyes back to his face, but his grin told her he knew exactly where her mind had been.

He took a step closer and Allie's mouth went dry.

"So, Allie, what exactly do you plan on doing with the rest of your night?"

"That, Logan, is none of your business."

He pursed his lips, as if considering her words, and Allie felt her eyes widen as he took a step closer. His body wasn't touching hers, but she could feel the heat radiating from him and it made her want to lean closer.

He raised his hand and ran it through her hair, and she couldn't think of one damn word to say. He looked at her, blue eyes penetrating.

He's going to kiss me, she thought. She knew she should be annoyed. She didn't even know him, but there was no denying the butterflies in her stomach or the goosebumps rising on her flesh. He flashed that damn mischievous smile again.

"Peanut shell," he said pulling something from her hair.

That was *not* a prickle of disappointment, she told herself. She wouldn't have let him kiss her anyway. He was a stranger, and *even she* knew better than to make out with strangers outside of dive bars.

"Well, like I said, I should get going. Sorry about…everything."

She turned and started to walk up the wet sidewalk toward her hotel. She was not using her best judgment, and probably ought to get away from this guy before she did something stupid.

"That's it? I thought after getting me punched in the face and spilling my drink, you'd at least offer to buy me dinner."

She glanced over her shoulder, but didn't stop walking. "Something tells me that's not the first time you've been punched in the face. And it's probably not going to be the last."

"True. But it might be the first time it was undeserved. I usually have it coming." He fell into step beside her.

"That part I believe. But I bet if you think hard enough, you can come up with a reason. Karma's funny that way."

Logan smiled again. "That's an interesting point. And probably true. So, no dinner?"

"Definitely not. I don't make a habit of buying dinner for strangers who follow me down dark streets in the middle of the night." Allie looked at him pointedly.

He held up his hands in mock surrender. "Am I giving off a stalker vibe? Cause I can go. It's just that this isn't the best neighborhood. And a young, ridiculously attractive person shouldn't be walking down dark streets in the middle of the night all alone."

Allie turned her head quick, but her smile was quicker. "Ridiculously attractive, huh? That's sweet, but I can take care of myself."

"I was talking about me. I've already been assaulted once tonight. Not sure I can handle another incident like that."

She couldn't stop the laugh. It bubbled up in her chest and she lowered her head as it escaped. "I see. So, you need a bodyguard?"

"A bodyguard makes me sound like a wimp. I prefer to think of it as employing the buddy system."

"I see your point," Allie said throwing him a sideways glance. "But this is my stop. Do you think you can manage the rest of the way on your own?" She glanced up at the three-story hotel where she was staying, in absolutely no hurry to go inside.

"I'm not sure. I should probably be under observation for at least thirty minutes, just to rule out a concussion. Don't you think?"

"Well, I definitely wouldn't want you to drop dead the second you stepped in your front door."

"Worried about me?" Logan asked.

"No, it's just that people saw us leave together. I'd be questioned and I have a busy day tomorrow."

Logan smiled again and that damn dimple in his cheek reappeared and made her lose her train of thought.

"There's a bar in this hotel," he said. "It's still early. I could buy you a drink to make up for the fact that you're stuck in my company for a little longer."

"It'll take more than a drink to make up for that. And I think you're underestimating your ability to annoy me if you think that will solve the problem." Allie looked up at him and smiled. She wobbled on her heels again, and this time she didn't think it had anything to do with the alcohol or the boots. He held out his arm and she took it. Oh yes, he was trouble. No doubt about it.

~

An hour later Allie and Logan were sitting in a corner booth at the bar. They'd agreed to just one more drink each, and it seemed neither of them was in a hurry to finish. Allie wanted to have her wits about her. Logan was too good looking, and he could charm the claws off a lobster. She didn't trust herself to make good choices around him, but she was having fun. She didn't want the night to end too soon.

It was hard to believe, but they had been talking non-stop the entire time. Conversation came easy with him. She told him about her little photo studio, and how she was carving out a living for herself doing what she loved. She told him about her house and the special place she lived—Big Falls—and how legend had it the town chose its residents. People Big Falls wanted to keep always wound up staying. And people she didn't like couldn't shake her dust off their boots fast enough. She was a living entity, Big Falls, Oklahoma. Allie told him all that, and more. She would talk until she ran out of things to say and then he would ask another question and she'd start talking all over again.

"So, you're in town to visit your brother and he stood you up?" Logan asked after another lull in the conversation.

"Not entirely his fault. He's the responsible one. Responsible people always get stuck with the last-minute crises."

Logan smiled. "I bet he wouldn't be very happy if he knew you were here with me instead."

He was looking deep into her eyes and Allie took a sip of her drink, feeling suddenly self-conscious. "Probably not, but he wouldn't be too shocked either."

"Really? So, you do this a lot?"

Allie laughed. "*No*. Never, actually. But he doesn't know that. My family is convinced that I'm only capable of making bad decisions."

"You have to admit, bad decisions are much more fun than good ones."

"I'll have to take your word on that. Contrary to what my family thinks, I've been very careful to avoid bad decisions for the last couple of years."

"And why is that?"

Allie took a slow sip and thought about her answer.

"When I was a kid, I think I just craved attention. When we were younger, my sister was always the brainy one, and my brother was the star athlete, and I didn't really have a *thing*. So, I became the troublemaker. But then everyone's lives got crazy. My brother was gone all the time, and my sister lost her husband. I was needed. So, I stepped up. I *grew* up. But it's hard to get my family to see that," she sighed. "How about you? Are you the doting son or the black sheep?"

The smile disappeared from his face.

"Let's not talk about my family."

"Why not? Is it that bad?"

"I don't want you to think I'm telling you some sob story just to get sympathy." He smiled again, but the sparkle was gone from his eyes and Allie found herself wishing it would come back.

"You don't need my sympathy." Allie inched closer to Logan.

in the round booth.

"Why's that?" Logan asked. The sexy smile returned to his face. The dimple reappeared and Allie let out a sigh.

"You made those bad decisions sound like so much fun, I think I might want to try one."

Logan leaned in close and his fingers twined in her hair. His lips brushed across hers and her mouth tingled. He pulled back a little, looking at her, waiting for her to react.

She knew what she *should* do. She *should* run back to her hotel room, bolt the door and sleep until this particular bad decision no longer seemed like a good idea. She stared into Logan's deep blue eyes and knew that wasn't going to happen. All her common sense was gone.

She smiled and raised her lips to his. She pressed her body closer. He kissed her, soft and sweet. His lips were warm on hers, gentle and tender. But she didn't want tender. Not tonight. She wanted something to make her forget her sister's broken heart, her nephew's shattered childhood, and the gaping whole Jeff's death had left in their family, to make her forget how it was tearing out her heart to see her brother leave them from the same airport, heading for the same destination.

As if reading her mind, Logan turned his head, angled his mouth across hers and kissed her like she'd never been kissed before. A tingle of anticipation swirled in her stomach. She didn't want to feel sad or afraid tonight, and she knew that if she let him, Logan would keep her too busy for any of those thoughts to enter her mind. He could make her forget, for a little while. If she let him, he could make her forget. And that was exactly what she was going to do.

She placed a hand on his chest, pushed him gently backward and said the first thing that popped into her head. "Wanna walk me to my room?"

Baby By Christmas

ALSO AVAILABLE

The McIntyre Men
Oklahoma Christmas Blues
Oklahoma Moonshine
Oklahoma Starshine
Shine On Oklahoma
Baby By Christmas
Oklahoma Sunshine

The Oklahoma Brands
The Brands who Came for Christmas
Brand-New Heartache
Secrets and Lies
A Mommy For Christmas
One Magic Summer
Sweet Vidalia Brand

ABOUT THE AUTHOR

New York Times and *USA Today* bestselling novelist Maggie Shayne has published sixty-two novels and twenty-two novellas for five major publishers over the course of twenty-two years. She also spent a year writing for American daytime TV dramas *The Guiding Light* and *As the World Turns*, and was offered the position of co-head writer of the former; a million-dollar offer she tearfully turned down. It was scary, turning down an offer that big. But her heart was in her books, and she'd found it impossible to do both.

In March 2014, she did something even scarier. She left the world's largest publisher and went "indie."

Now, she is embarking on an exciting new leg of her publishing journey, with most of her titles moving to small press publisher, Oliver Heber Books.

Maggie writes small town contemporary romances like the recent *Bliss in Big Falls* series, which boasts "a miracle in every story."

She cut her teeth on western themed category romances like her classic 90s and early 2000s *The Texas Brand* and *The Oklahoma All-Girl Brands,* and later expanded into romantic suspense and thrillers like *The Secrets of Shadow Falls* and *The Brown and de Luca Novels.*

She is perhaps best known for her beloved paranormal romances, like the brand new *Fatal series* and perennial favorites *The Immortals,* the *By Magic series*, and *Wings in the Night.*

Maggie is a fifteen-time RITA® Award nominee and one-time winner. She lives in the rolling green and forested hilltops of Cortland County NY, wine & dairy country, despite having sworn off both. She is a vegan Wiccan hippy living her best life with her beloved husband Lance, and usually at least two dogs.

Maggie also writes spiritual self-help and runs an online magic shop, BlissBlog.org

Visit Maggie at www.maggieshayne.com

CPSIA information can be obtained
at www.ICGtesting.com
Printed in the USA
LVHW091408070423
743785LV00024B/283

9 781648 392986